THE EMPEROR REVERSES TIME

그 황제가 시곗바늘을 되돌린 사연

WRITTEN BY BLOOMING BOUQUET

EDITIO

PUBLISHING

The Emperor Reverses Time

© Blooming Bouquet

Cover Illustration by SAELAH

This is a work of fiction. Names, characters, businesses, places, events, locales, and incidents are either the products of the author's imagination or used in a fictitious manner. Any resemblance to actual persons, living or dead, or actual events is purely coincidental.

The views and opinions expressed in this work are those of the author and do not necessarily reflect the views and opinions of Editio Publishing, LLC.

그 황제가 시곗바늘을 되돌린 사연 by Blooming Bouquet

Copyright © 2021 by Blooming Bouquet
Cover Illustration Rights © 2020 SAELAH

All rights reserved.

This English edition was published by Editio Publishing LLC in 2025 by exclusive contract with Kyobo Book Centre Co. Ltd.

ISBN 978-1-959742-67-8 (Print)

Printed in the United States of America

https://editiopublishing.com/

The Emperor Reverses Time

CONTENTS

This work contains descriptions of child abuse.

BETWEEN THAT SPRING AND SUMMER

CHAPTER
THIRTY-ONE

Elizabeth opened her journal. The journal that Leonhardt had given her shortly after she entered the imperial palace. It was made of a smooth, gray-pink leather, with Elizabeth's initials and the imperial family's symbol on the cover.

What should I write in this?

Just write anything you want. What you did today and how you felt when you did it, or what you want to do tomorrow...

When she had first heard that, Elizabeth had begun writing about the day they first met. She had been writing in the diary every day since.

Elizabeth chewed on the tip of her pen and suddenly felt startled by how unladylike her behavior was. She quickly looked around to make sure no one was watching before putting the pen tip in her mouth again. Such behavior would have been unthinkable just three months ago. However, now Elizabeth knew that no one would scold or reprimand her for behaving unlike a lady should.

So, is it fine as long as no one is watching? Elizabeth wondered as she, lost in her memories with the pen tip in her mouth, began to flip through the thick pages.

[I met Leon for the first time. I was so nervous and made a lot of mistakes, but Leon didn't scold me and treated me kindly.]

[Leon gave me shoes with no heels. Everything felt so new; I could feel a soft sensation along with crunching sounds whenever I walked on the lawn. As I started running, my hair fluttered in the wind. He proposed to me with a flower ring. I was so happy I cried.]

At that time, she hadn't known that people cry when they are happy.

Elizabeth smiled bitterly as she continued to flip the pages.

[Thanks to His Majesty and Her Majesty, as well as Leon, I can live in the imperial palace. I was so nervous because it was an unfamiliar place, but I felt a bit relieved because Leon was there.]

[This time, Leon made me a crown using flowers. He said that he'll bring a veil next time... will he really? Leon really can do anything. I want to grow into an excellent lady who doesn't bring any shame to him or his family. I dried the flower crown prettily with the maids' help and put it at the head side of my bed.]

Even now, that flower crown was still at the head of her bed, giving her nice dreams with its fragrant scent.

[Leon got me a puppy. His name is Bailey. He's white, black, pink, and right now he's biting on my slippers. He keeps on causing trouble every day, but I always feel like smiling whenever I see him. Is this what it means to find something cute?]

"Bailey! You took my cushion again! No, give it to me!"

Whenever Bailey was quiet, there were only two possible reasons. Either he was sleeping, or he was sneaking around about to cause trouble.

Elizabeth sensed something and quickly turned around to shout at Bailey, who had grown as big as the two largest pillows on her bed. Pouting, Bailey dropped the cushion he had been drenching with drool. But Elizabeth was no longer fooled by that face. She put her hands on her waist and scolded him again. Bailey whined as he rested his chin on the cushion and lay down.

[*For the first time ever, someone made a dress with no corset just for me. I met my guard knight, Sir Bern. It was all thanks to Leon's consideration.*]

[*The day we went to the Clock Tower. I met Big Sis Mimir. I heard that Leon went through a hard time because of my careless actions. Big Sis Mimir said that all magic requires a price. I've reflected on my actions and will never do it again.*]

[*His Majesty the Emperor held a welcoming reception for me.*]

Elizabeth's hand stopped flipping the pages. The symptoms were appearing again. Whenever Elizabeth remembered the things that happened at the welcoming reception, her face began to burn, and the room would turn suddenly hot.

[*Leon returned the flower ring he borrowed. Along with a wonderful interest. And then he asked for my permission. Just what exactly is happiness that Leon would ask for my permission that eagerly? I'm still not sure.*]

She reached for the bouquet in the crystal vase. The other flowers were already withered and had a preservation magic cast on them, but the violet made from amethyst and the forget-me-not of blue sapphire still sparkled.

[*The feeling I had when father and mother hugged me, when Leon hugged me, and when Her Majesty the Empress hugged me, were all different. I don't know what the difference is. Compared to the empress' or Leon's embrace, father and mother's hugs don't feel as nice.*]

Elizabeth rubbed her forearm. She was only reminiscing about it, but she still felt uncomfortable and got the creeps.

She realized then, looking at the pages, that she had begun every sentence with Leonhardt's name. Quickly, Elizabeth closed her journal before anyone could see.

Tingly and fluttery. Lately, just thinking about Leonhardt worsened the shivering feelings in her heart. Elizabeth pressed the back of her hand to her cheek and leaned her face against the cool wooden desk. Her burning cheek felt much cooler being pressed against the cold wood.

She'd already consulted the maids and Leonhardt's nanny, the doctor, and the history teacher, and even Her Majesty the Empress about this symptom. However, whenever she did, they would just smile and send her away, saying that she would understand one day.

The maids gave her chocolate, the doctor gave her a candy that would prevent cavities, and the history teacher talked to her about his old love story. Her Majesty even went as far as making eye contact with His Majesty the Emperor, who was next to her, and exchanged a light kiss right then and there.

When I told Leon about it, he got angry and said, "What exactly are father and mother doing in front of a child..."

Why did he do that? Elizabeth chewed on the pen tip again as she tried her best to understand. She rested her chin on the desk and thought back on the welcoming reception and ball again.

Elizabeth took the bouquet Leonhardt was holding for her. The crowd offered heartwarming smiles, looking on at the adorable young pair. The moment she took the bouquet and nodded, Leonhardt made a deeply moved expression as if a god had just given him forgiveness.

Elizabeth didn't understand why he made that expression. It seemed as though making someone happy was so difficult and challenging that it required permission... By grasping it like that, Elizabeth decided that she would do her best to be happy to help Leonhardt.

After giving her the present, Leonhardt then Elizabeth for a dance. Since she was today's guest of honor, it was only right that she started the dance. Elizabeth moved with perfect steps and graceful twirls. Her skirt billowed like a rose in full bloom and settled slowly like a dandelion puff.

Leonhardt moved with the music with incredible discipline to match her movements, to the point that no one would believe that he was a child who just got drenched with alcohol from head to toe.

It was the best courtesy he could and should do for a lady who had yet to make her official debut in society.

Elizabeth's next dance partner was the empress. Elizabeth was about to carefully reach out to the hand the emperor was holding out, but the empress snatched her away with a mischievous smile. She taught her a new lively dance to match the current music with a fast tempo.

Even after they finished dancing to one more song, the emperor had to wait until the music calmed some, to save his dignity. After dancing with His Majesty the Emperor, it was her guard knight Sir Bern's turn. Dancing with all these important figures made Elizabeth feel proud.

Although thinking about it now, the adults were only matching her small figure and just moved their body left and right in place...

"But what is so important about steps and movements when it is just fun to hold hands and spin?" Leonhardt muttered as he held onto Elizabeth's hand. Mimir nodded in agreement as she held onto Elizabeth's other hand.

With Leonhardt and Mimir in both hands, she very much enjoyed dancing to the song with a fast and cheerful tempo by spinning together with all the other noble children. The music filled her heart, and a wide smile spread across her face.

Knock, knock, knock.

"Lizzie, are you there?" It was Leonhardt's voice.

Elizabeth gasped, stood upright, and shoved her diary inside her bookshelf before opening the door.

"You were late, so I thought something happened..."

"Mm, it's nothing. I was just looking at my diary."

"Your diary?"

Elizabeth nodded. Before her, Leonhardt stood clad in white formal attire. Taking the hand Leonhardt held out to her, they made their way to the anteroom where the empress, her tailor, and the maids were waiting.

"Then, I'll see you later." Leonhardt placed a kiss on Elizabeth's forehead before handing her over to the maids. Both she and Elizabeth had grown these last few months, but Elizabeth was still a finger joint taller than Leonhardt, so he had to stand on tiptoe to kiss her.

Should I really drink more milk? No, I need to work out to get stronger and taller... Is my workout the problem? Leonhardt pondered.

Waving goodbye as Leonhardt walked away, Elizabeth suddenly exclaimed when she spotted the dress the tailor had brought. "How beautiful!"

"I should be the one to thank you for making me happy again this time. But this dress is..."

"Still incomplete, right?"

The tailor and Elizabeth exchanged looks before laughing.

The first time they met, the tailor couldn't imagine that the girl could laugh like this. She looked so perfect and doll like, yet so awkward. But now, she smiled so naturally, just like the girl in the tailor's sketches. The tailor secretly sniffled when she thought about how surprised and thankful she was for Elizabeth's transformation.

The large, puffy sleeves featured fabric roses, each accented with white pearls and lace details. The skirt, woven of silken fabric and embroidered with silver thread in the shape of roses, was deliberately slit so that the six-tiered lace frill petticoat could be seen under the white ribbon adornment. Around the neckline, gemstones glittered like floating petals, arranged in a design that resembled a round clamshell.

Instead of gloves, fake flowers with ribbons dangling around were tied as wristbands. An imperial jewel sparkled on Elizabeth's neck. Finally, she put on a pair of shoes that, once again, Leonhardt had personally selected. The elegant shoes featured short, precise heels and were adorned with silk flowers, each centered with diamonds. Their shine made them seem to be made of fairy wings. Every step she took seemed to leave a trail of rainbows.

"How pretty. My daughter-in-law, will you come here?"

"Yes, Your Majesty."

The empress hadn't stopped smiling ever since Elizabeth had come into the anteroom. Beaming at her, the empress hugged Elizabeth tightly. She asked, "Leon said he wanted to put the last decoration on you. Is that okay?"

"Leon did...?"

The empress nodded. Elizabeth tilted her head as she vaguely thought about how anything Leon gave her was always good, so she gave her consent.

"Then, Lizzie, I'm coming in, okay?" Leonhardt entered the anteroom carrying a flower crown made out of summer roses that just recently bloomed in the empress' garden.

"Leon! That flower crown is..."

Leonhardt stood on tiptoe and placed the flower crown on Elizabeth's head. He even put a small veil on it with the help of the maids.

"That time... I told you that I would get a veil next time, right? I always keep my promises." Leonhardt's voice cracked a bit.

Elizabeth's eyes blinked wide eyes in a daze. The thing that she just read in her diary came true right in front of her eyes.

"It suits you well. You're very pretty as well today, Lizzie," Leonhardt said with a smile for Elizabeth.

Elizabeth, who had no idea how grateful he was to God and how thankful he was to the witch of the Clock Tower, became red in the face and could only cover her cheeks with her hands as she stamped her feet.

"Then, my sweethearts, shall we go now?"

Elizabeth held Leonhardt's and the empress' hands, smiling as they headed towards the church inside the imperial palace.

Today, the day before summer, Elizabeth Isolde von Elysium and Leonhardt Tristan von Esphedor were going to promise their futures to each other in the presence of God.

CHAPTER
THIRTY-TWO

The futures they promised each other were nourished with each joyful moment. Of course, not every day was as joyful as a dream. The day Leonhardt's voice broke for the first time, Elizabeth was sincerely worried that he had contracted some kind of illness. Meanwhile, Leonhardt was sincerely disappointed that he couldn't sing for her for a while.

Knock, knock, knock.

"Lizzie?"

Elizabeth made the knocking sounds with her voice before entering Leonhardt's chamber like it was natural. She was wearing a blue linen dress with laces knitted in the shape of flowers along the hem of her skirt and a silk ribbon of her favorite flowers embroidered on her chest. She wore ankle-length lace socks and a pair of smooth black shoes.

Seeing how she had grown, Leonhardt was deeply moved. Over the years, she always seemed to grow a finger's length taller than Leonhardt. Every time that happened, Leonhardt was thrilled that she was growing well, and

Elizabeth said she hoped Leon would grow as big as Albert soon.

And then I used to tease her by asking if Sir Bern appeared in her dreams as a crush...

It had stung a bit that his fiancée's first love wasn't him, but rather a man who was a head taller than his peers and resembled a knight on a white horse. He had the knight's signature golden hair and blue eyes—and was a real knight—but that was old news.

A month ago, that man had officially married a lady chosen by his house, and they had just returned from a happy honeymoon.

"What's wrong?" Elizabeth's blue eyes sparkled as she grinned.

It was a magical smile that could even make the guards protecting the emperor's chambers smile along.

"I just miss you." Leonhardt grinned too.

Other young girls attended etiquette classes to become perfect ladies day by day, but his lovely fiancée here before him seemed more and more like an untethered bird, one flying free as she roamed the imperial palace with a spring in her step.

Yet, no one in this imperial palace would stop or berate her for doing that. Even if she were to come out to dance in the garden under the rain in the middle of the night wearing only her sleepwear, no one would stop her. Rather, they would prepare a warm bath and a hot tea for her when she came back drenched all over.

"What are you doing, Leon?"

"Oh... umm... reminiscing about our engagement ceremony? The weather that day was as bright as today, after all. It was also right between spring and summer, and you were..."

"I was?" Elizabeth's blue eyes twinkled with expectation. This was a conversation that they'd gone through multiple times already, but every time, her eyes sparkled, and her cheeks turned pink.

"Cute and lovely, obviously."

"Then what about now?"

Leonhardt carefully grabbed Elizabeth's hand and looked her in the eyes. "Even more beautiful, and more lovely, of course."

Elizabeth giggled with her unique, clear voice. This conversation, a small and secret language they promised each other, was something no adult would understand and one she would never tire of.

Leonhardt slightly tickled Elizabeth's palm with his fingertips before asking, "What did you do today?"

"I made a floral arrangement with Her Majesty the Empress. I even got complimented that I'm already quite skilled at it now."

"I can bet my snack today that it will be placed in father's bedchamber within the day."

"Oh my gosh! I would've arranged it with my whole heart if I'd known!" Contrary to her words, Elizabeth had a grin on her face.

"No wonder you had the scent of flowers on you. Lizzie, you... always appear in front of me looking like a fairy, you know that?"

"Then am I a flower fairy today? Can I take care of all the flowers in the imperial palace later when I become the empress?"

Hearing that, Leonhardt made a very serious face. He didn't do it to tease Elizabeth, but he was really seriously thinking about it. *Can I really not change the predetermined fate?*

He was concerned about the conversation he had with the master of the Clock Tower on the day she vanished into the clock, during which he unsparingly gave as much of his own lifespan as the time she spent inside to save her.

"Leon?"

"If you want to, not just the imperial palace, I can even arrange it so you can take care of all the flowers in the entire empire." Leonhardt shifted his expression into a bright smile as he held Elizabeth's hand.

It didn't matter whether fate was predetermined, or they had to make their own from now on. The only thing that mattered to him was Elizabeth's happiness. For the sake of that, he wouldn't mind turning back time over and over again—no matter the price.

"Lady Elizabeth, His Majesty has inquired if he could move the flowers you arranged today to his chambers because it is to his fancy. What would you like to do?"

The maid's words made Elizabeth and Leonhardt exchange glances again. If the emperor wanted to, he could just take her flowers without saying anything, but he would always ask for her opinion like this first.

"I'm glad that His Majesty doesn't think that it would sully his chambers since I'm still lacking, but I would love to give it to him as much as he wants."

The maid made a courteous bow and disappeared with quick steps.

"What is today's snack again?" Leonhardt asked, shrugging.

Elizabeth stood up, frowning. "I'll get the snack tomorrow. I planned to have a teatime with Big Sis Mimir after this."

"Mimir again? Are you still doing weird things with Mimir because you want to learn magic?"

"What weird things...? We're just going to have a normal teatime between ladies today. It's nothing a gentleman should bother with!" Elizabeth was determined to have no aptitude for magic by Mimir Brunnr, but Mimir gritted her teeth and said that she would teach her magic no matter how.

This was how they kept experiencing miserable failures. And the youngest magicians of the Clock Tower and Leonhardt were always the ones cleaning up after their mistakes. But it was a relief that they were not doing any of that today. Even if Leonhardt felt relieved, in one corner of his heart, he began to worry that Mimir might brew the tea with the hind legs of a frog or a dried spiderweb.

He said, "If you say so, then I shall obey, my lady. Take care. Don't eat anything strange, don't get lost..."

"Your Highness the Crown Prince, I am already seventeen, you know?" Elizabeth pouted as she took out her pocket watch. It was the watch that Mimir gave her at her welcoming reception.

Leonhardt just smiled and waved his hand. Elizabeth used the watch and disappeared before his eyes in an instant.

Lizzie is already seventeen... Leonhardt put his hands together to hold up his head, putting aside the pile of homework behind him and leaning his back on the chair.

A lot of things happened in the last few years.

The studies he went through for the second time were still difficult. Even though he had surely learned them before, when he started studying again, he felt that it was unfamiliar and difficult—like he was learning it for the first time.

To think I would be learning this at this age. This is unforgivable. Leonhardt grumbled in front of the teaching materials, which gave him headaches just from the titles.

But Leonhardt's teacher always shook his head. *Your Highness, the marquis of Perian's young lord finished all these books when he was ten years old. The person who will become this nation's emperor should not say something so feeble.*

Hearing that, Leonhardt could only shut his mouth.

Isn't it around this summer when I'm supposed to officially meet that guy, Ils? When he closed his eyes, he could vividly remember his face admonishing him with his life on the line, questioning how he could do that as a person. He was someone who would react sensitively to trivial things like a rabbit and would rarely raise his voice, and yet for that moment, he sincerely got angry.

That shows how unforgivable and horrible I must've seemed to him... Leonhardt hit his head against the desk as he took a deep breath. *I want to thank him if I could meet him again, but...*

Judging by his personality, if he were thanked by the Crown Prince at their first meeting, he would be so surprised he might pass out. Leonhardt shook his head as he looked outside the window.

The summer sun cast a warm yellow light through the wavering shade of the clouds.

Huh? Elizabeth returned to the palace after a pleasant teatime with Mimir, walking lightly down the hill where unknown flowers bloomed. She stopped walking when she saw a white and fluffy lump-like thing from afar.

Bailey...?

The white lump was circling around the lake surrounding the Clock Tower.

Elizabeth approached it, thinking that Bailey might have lost his way and ran after her all the way here.

However, what she found wasn't Bailey. It was a boy.

His hair was as white as snow. It was long enough to reach right below his shoulders, but it was tied up. His eyes were so red they reminded her of the red roses that had decorated the flower vase this morning. At first glance, the boy looked her age.

This was the first time Elizabeth ever met someone her age inside the imperial palace other than Leonhardt, so she gathered her courage and said, "Excuse me..."

The boy, who lugged a large book in his arms while pacing back and forth, jumped a little as he turned to face her.

Elizabeth thought that he looked just like a startled rabbit. She tried, "Are you... trying to go to the tower?"

The boy nodded as an answer to her question. "But I'm not sure how to go to that tower... I would've been able to go somehow if there were a boat..."

Elizabeth blinked at him. The shirt the boy was wearing had long sleeves, so the sleeve on his arm that was carrying the book was sliding down. But the boy's arms looked too slender and weak to row a boat. Elizabeth didn't know much about nautical skills, but she could at least figure that part out.

"What business do you have in the tower?" Elizabeth moved toward the boy, just a little closer.

His shoulders flinched, but he replied, "I-I want to meet my teacher." The boy held the book in front of his face like a shield.

Elizabeth tilted her head and questioned again, "Teacher?"

The boy nodded.

"Is your teacher inside the tower?"

He nodded again.

Elizabeth pondered this. The tower in the middle of the lake was a space for magicians, and people who weren't magicians needed a boat to go to the tower. But not even a board was at the dock, much less a boat. And even if there was a boat, the only thing they could do was stand still on the boat so it wouldn't overturn. She didn't know what emergency the boy had, but he kept on pacing, looking increasingly desperate.

Elizabeth took out her pocket watch. She said, "I'll help you."

"Y-you will? Are you also... a magician like Miss Mimir?" The boy's round, red eyes got even bigger.

"Do you know Big Sis Mimir?"

"She is my teacher's granddaughter... Oooh!"

Elizabeth grinned when she heard a familiar name come out of an unfamiliar boy's mouth. She then grabbed the boy's hand and used the watch to take him to the tower.

"Big Sis Mimir!"

"Elizabeth? You...!"

"Miss Mimir? Oh my goodness, how is this possible?"

Mimir, who was stirring a large pot by standing on thick books instead of a platform, spun around. She had just been about to check whether Elizabeth had left the Clock Tower safely, but her mana once again shook and brought the two people into her room.

Elizabeth smiled, amused by the pots, cups, and plates with leftover cake cream, along with the table and chairs, somewhat stuck in the corner of the ceiling. No matter how many times she saw it, it was really a convenient and amusing magic. *If only I knew how to use magic like that, I could've hidden Bailey's snacks with that skill...*

The boy sat on the ground rather awkwardly, looking puzzled as he examined his surroundings.

"Elizabeth, did you forget something? That kid is...?"

Mimir looked at Elizabeth and the boy one after the other.

THIRTY-THREE

Elizabeth started to explain the situation in a voice that gradually turned into a murmur, "He said he had to go to the Clock Tower... but there's no boat... so, I used the pocket watch you gave me..."

What if Big Sis gets angry? If she asks to return the pocket watch... that means she doesn't want to see me again... I don't want that... but I was the wrong one for using the pocket watch as I pleased. Elizabeth felt her hands tremble, her cheeks go hot with anxiety.

After looking alternately at Elizabeth and the little rabbit-like boy who didn't seem to grasp what was happening, Mimir nodded like she just remembered something.

"Now that I think about it, today is that day! Sorry, Ils. I completely forgot since I was too focused on my research." Mimir clapped her hands before jumping down the pile of books she had been using as a platform. "Grandfather is inside. Do you want me to lead you there?"

The boy stood and brushed the dust off his clothes, nodding.

"Lizzie, can you wait here for a moment? I'll be back soon!" As Mimir gently swung her hand at the air, rainbow flowers and butterflies began to fall in front of Elizabeth like snow.

Oh, thinking back, I haven't even heard his name, Elizabeth thought. Maybe it didn't matter? Elizabeth tilted her head as she waved her hand towards Mimir, who disappeared holding the rabbit-boy's hand.

She had said she would be back soon, but even after Elizabeth took a nap leaning against the pile of books, Mimir still hadn't returned. The rainbow flowers and butterflies still flitted around her, but even watching that had become boring for her. Elizabeth stretched and fixed her messy hair, before standing up.

Would the Elizabeth, who had lived at the duke's residence, believe she would become friends with the witch of the Clock Tower if someone told her? That she would loaf around and nap on that friend's dusty carpet? Elizabeth giggled as she brushed the dust from her clothes. She looked around for a paper and pen that would be safe for her to use.

Elizabeth left a memo in handwriting more graceful than an adult's, promising she would return to play before using the pocket watch again. It was almost time for Leonhardt to come back after his sword training. After his sword training, Leonhardt always enjoyed plentiful snacks with Elizabeth. For her, a time like this was a special part of the day.

"Sir Bern!"

"Lady Elizabeth. Welcome aboard." Albert greeted the girl as she ran over.

"Where is Leon?" Elizabeth asked her knight Albert, thinking that she couldn't see Leonhardt around because she was a bit late after having to run back to the Clock Tower earlier.

Albert offered Elizabeth his arm. His clothes had folds from having to bend a little to match her height every time he escorted her, but Albert thought of them as a sort of badge of honor. He said, "His Highness is currently changing his clothes after finishing his training. How did you spend time today, my lady?"

"I went to the Clock Tower for a bit. Oh right! I heard that helping people in need is included in chivalry. Does that mean I'm also a knight?"

Albert blinked. It was hard for him to understand what the girl, who had wrists thinner than the handle of the spear the knights used, was talking about. "Umm... what kind of help did you do?"

"I helped a person who wanted to go to the Clock Tower but was troubled because he couldn't find a boat." Elizabeth announced triumphantly.

Albert smiled as he thought about how admirable and adorable the girl was. "I see you did something good. Lady Elizabeth is already an amazing knight."

"Oh my, really?" Elizabeth was sincerely happy. In her eyes, the knights always looked neat, spoke politely, treated her with manners like they would to a respectable lady—tall, suited in white uniforms, and they were already married... No, that wasn't the point.

The knights in the imperial palace had always been the objects of Elizabeth's admiration.

"Lizzie?" Leonhardt widened his eyes as he saw Elizabeth being led into the training ground by Albert. He had just roughly wiped his sweaty body with a wet towel after his training and was about to change his clothes.

"Leon! Oh, excuse me, sorry!"

The moment Elizabeth noticed that he was in the middle of changing, she stopped herself from running towards him and stormed outside again instead.

"Lady Elizabeth?"

"Y-yes?"

Leonhardt's half naked—or half clothed—appearance was floating in front of her. His hair soaked with sweat, his calm violet gaze that she rarely saw because he was always smiling when they were together, his slightly drooping lip shape, and his side profile that showed a clear line along the shadows that went down from his forehead to his jaw. His well-trained muscles had begun to settle in his youthful body, which looked so strong it was hard to tell that he was still a teenager. However, when she looked closely, he still had thin and slender lines.

Just like what the knights were saying, he might really become a sword master. Elizabeth tried to imagine Leonhardt as a sword master while she was waiting for him. She felt like her object of admiration wouldn't be knights anymore, but Leonhardt.

"You should've waited ahead in the palace."

"But I wanted to see Leon."

Leonhardt, at a loss for words, just stared at her in a daze. The empress that he read about in the diary never tried to find him first no matter how much she wanted to see him. She was a foolishly quiet and shy person whose heart fluttered just passing him by for a second or holding hands with him for show at official functions. Yet, here she was, telling him she wanted to see him and even came to find him.

"Leon... are you crying?"

"N-no! There's just... dust coming into my eyes... Let's head back now."

Was I always this bad at controlling my emotions? Leonhardt complained to himself about his adolescent emotions as he grabbed Elizabeth's hand.

"Then, I'll see you tomorrow."

"Good work, everyone." Albert smiled fondly as he watched the two heading to the main palace hand in hand. No wonder that all kinds of flowers seemed to bloom exceptionally beautifully this summer. The very reason was right there.

Outside on the lawn, in the warmth of the sun, they spread out a red-checkered picnic blanket for lunch. While they were waiting for the maids to come bearing the picnic basket, Leonhardt lay down on it and was about to doze off. The warm wind wafted gently over them.

Elizabeth, who had gotten used to spending every day with a smile, sat down next to him, and started chattering about her day like a mountain bird. Her laughter sounded sweet and bell-like.

It was about time for the picnic basket made with the kitchen's heart and soul to come.

If heaven were real, it would probably be this place, Leonhardt thought.

"Leon, did a guest come to the imperial palace?"

"A guest?"

"Yes. I met someone I just saw for the first time, you see. His height was around Leon's height, he was carrying this big book, and..."

Leonhardt straightened up when he heard that. There was one person that came to mind.

"Could it be... a boy who has white hair and red eyes like a rabbit?"

"Do you know him?"

Leonhardt nodded. He was confident that this was someone he knew the best in the whole world.

"In the welcoming reception back then, there was no child who could be our friend... or rather, there were a lot of happenings that made us unable to make friends. That's why father and mother personally selected noble children of our age who could be our friends and summoned them to the palace. He's probably one of them."

The maids gently placed the picnic basket between the two of them. The basket made of reeds was divided into three tiers. Each section was filled with small dishes as if it were a children's house play set. Those dishes, once used for playing house a few years ago, were now used by respectable adults and placed inside the basket.

Leonhardt scratched his cheek, feeling jittery when he thought about how much they had grown.

Sandwiches baked with plenty of butter, a steaming roast beef, and a cake topped with strawberries over white cream were placed one by one on the blue plates being served on the picnic mat. After drawing a serene flower pattern on a white background and filling the gold-rimmed teacups with well-brewed black tea instead of milk tea, the maids took their leave again.

"About that white-haired kid."

"Hm?" Elizabeth turned her gaze to him, trying to take a careful bite on the sandwich so its fillings wouldn't spill out.

Leonhardt pondered whether it would be right to speak of it, but he decided that it would be better for her to find out sooner rather than later. "Ilysses Eldirjan von Perian. He's the heir to the marquis of Perian." The marquis of Perian was one of the families that Elizabeth must've heard of before. "It'll be good to get along with him."

Elizabeth, still chewing on the sandwich, asked why with her eyes.

Instead of saying 'something will happen in the future and that boy will do this for you,' Leonhardt replied like a boy going through a stormy adolescence with his self-reflection. "Meeting someone who you can understand and can understand you more than anyone, and would give their all to stop a friend from going down the wrong path is a chance that not everyone has the luxury of having..."

Elizabeth tilted her head. Lately, Leonhardt had been setting the mood like this to say words she couldn't understand. "But Leon."

"Huh?"

"Aren't you eating the carrot?" Elizabeth blinked as she pointed at Leonhardt's plate.

The plate—which had held meat—now only had decorative flowers, carrots cut into the shape of rabbits, and broccoli left on the side.

"Mother said that if we leave food on our plate, we're going to have to eat it all mixed together when we die later..." Elizabeth slurred the end of her words on purpose, glancing at Leonhardt.

"I-is that so? Then should I start leaving candies or cakes on my plate from now on so the food mix will be a little tastier?"

"...Don't tell me Leon is unable to eat carrots?"

"As if! Why would I not be able to eat carrots? I just don't eat it!" Leonhardt immediately covered his mouth with his hand, realizing he might have said too much. There's a world of difference between not being able to eat something and choosing not to eat it.

Elizabeth gazed into Leonhardt's eyes with her own pure and innocent ones, captivating him completely. "I think Your Highness the Crown Prince is very amazing."

"R-really?" *Thanks for thinking that. Thank you, but...*

"To think the amazing His Highness doesn't eat carrots..."

"It's not like I don't eat it, I can eat it if I'm told to, so Lizzie, listen to me over here...!"

"It's a little disappointing. Now I understand why you've been growing as fast as me." Elizabeth teased Leonhardt with a big smile to her eyes.

Leonhardt dropped his fork.

To the maids who were watching the two from afar, they were just so adorable that they had to grab onto the pillar or pinch each other's sides to hold themselves back from smiling. But to Leonhardt, this was the biggest crisis of his nineteen years of life.

"I can eat it!"

"Really?" Elizabeth said, raising her eyebrows.

Leonhardt took a new fork as if he was flaunting, stabbed it to the flower-shaped carrot, and brought it closer to his mouth.

"I can... eat..." Contrary to his mind, his mouth wouldn't open.

Is this damn body for real? Even if my body is of a child, what's inside is a whole grownup, right?! No matter how bad a carrot tastes to a child's tongue, there's no way an adult can't eat carrots!

Leonhardt could feel cold sweat dripping over the back of his neck. Elizabeth watched him, casually munching on the rabbit-shaped carrots, smirking. "Oh dear, this can't do. Your Highness, will you come over here for a second?"

"...Lizzie, you've been acting like you're so grown up lately, huh?" Leonhardt put down his fork and scooted closer to Elizabeth.

"Now! Say ahh—" Elizabeth picked up the fork Leonhardt had just put down and stabbed all the remaining carrots. She held it toward Leonhardt.

Leonhardt couldn't even believe what he was seeing. If he could, he would've already digested the carrots already, yet now she stabbed each of them and made them into a lump. She was even pushing it into his mouth while saying such an embarrassing thing...

Is this a dream? But the rich smell of the meat sauce that pierced his nose made him realize that this was not a dream. Leonhardt alternately looked at the determined Elizabeth and the group of maids before closing his eyes and opening his mouth.

"Aww, good boy. Our Crown Prince eats so well! You're going to grow so big and strong!"

"Lizzie... I'm two years older than you, you know?"

Gulp. No matter how much he chewed, the taste of the carrots forcefully shoved into his mouth really didn't match his taste even as a young adult. Leonhardt rinsed his mouth with a juice made by squeezing fruits as he glared at Elizabeth, flustered.

Elizabeth just giggled sweetly.

To think the day would come where I would be fed carrots by my empress...

How sweet a person she was. Why didn't he know that she was friendly, pure, and such a bright person that it was like a bunch of daffodils would grow in full bloom around them whenever she smiled? Leonhardt reproached himself once again while Elizabeth was trying to feed him a slightly scorched broccoli after the carrot, as if she was playing house with him instead of a doll.

Do I have the right to eat this? In an instant, he felt disgusted at himself for opening his mouth obediently, chewing a few times to pretend he was eating something he didn't like, and looking for juice with a frown.

"Leon?"

Leonhardt's expression darkened.

Elizabeth called to him, sounding confused. "S-sorry. Did you get angry because I forced you to eat vegetables even though I didn't know how much you hate them...?"

"Huh? N-no. It's not like that. How can I ever get angry at you, Lizzie? Ah! I usually hate these vegetables so much, but they taste so much tastier because Lizzie fed me!"

Leonhardt smiled awkwardly as he tried to avoid the downcast Elizabeth's eyes.

"Oh, recently, Her Majesty the Empress said that..."

"Mother?"

When Elizabeth said that she heard the empress mutter that she wanted to go to the sea, Leonhardt squinted his eyes.

The sea? Why did she suddenly want to go to the sea? He got a bad feeling. Leonhardt forcefully shoved all the remaining vegetables into his mouth and swallowed hard.

THE SONG SUNG BY THE WAVES

THIRTY-FOUR

Freyja Ivanna von Esphedor was painting in the palace of the empress. On days when the sun shone and shimmered into a thousand rays of light through the clean glass windows, the empress sometimes set aside her schedule and took out canvas and paint. Even when the emperor entered the room, the empress' brush didn't stop moving. When she focused on painting, she noticed nothing else. The emperor knew that perfectly well, so he usually just sent away the maids with a gesture and sat on a chair to watch the empress.

In the shining sunlight, the empress kept her back straight as she made repeated, precise brushstrokes, her hand stained with paint, a satisfied smile on her face.

The emperor used his thumbs and forefingers to make a rectangular shape with his hand. Inside the frame he made was the sight he loved the most in the world. In other people's eyes, the empress would be described as someone who was beautiful, graceful, and elegant. However, with the empress so focused, her lips slightly open, sitting so close to the canvas holding her breath—this was a side of her that only he could see.

The only hobbies of the empress that other people knew were flower arrangement, painting, and poetry appreciation. In addition, the empress could embroider so well and in such a modest manner that all ladies attending a bride class admired her. She also read difficult philosophy books to gain the knowledge that the mother of the empire should have, and...

The emperor thought back to the hidden small saddle inside the empress' treasure box. He knew better than anyone how beautiful and bright the empress' face was when she enjoyed doing the things she really liked. And he also knew what pain was hiding behind that smile right now and how much she was slowly collapsing.

The previous empress—the emperor's mother and Freyja's mother-in-law—was as cold as the perpetual snow, stern, and fastidious. It would not be an exaggeration to say that, when she became the most elderly member of the imperial family, time seemed to have stopped within the imperial palace.

Flowerpots were always in the same place. Flowers matching the season would be arranged in the same shape every day inside the same vases. It was prohibited to mess up the tableware and even documents on her desk. Pictures in frames were never changed; the academic and philosophy books filling the study were never swapped for poetry books, and there were never any new kinds of flowers blooming in the garden.

She, who thought that waking up and starting the day at the same time every day was the most basic and natural thing in the world, breathed her last at the exact same time she usually went to sleep every day.

And then, Freyja Ivanna, the lady of a house that had always lived in the harbor, was unfortunately the most free-spirited girl in the empire to become the empress.

The emperor carefully approached the empress, who was so focused on the canvas in front of her that she hadn't noticed his arrival. When he looked closer at what she was painting, the emperor squinted his eyes. The sea portrayed in the painting was clearly the sea from her birthplace.

The first meeting of the two had been just like a fairytale. One day, out of nowhere, they found each other by chance. The then Crown Prince—who was enjoying a summer vacation in a coast famous for being the empire's most beautiful vacation spot, a hill where white flowers were in full bloom with the horizon in sight, and a beach abundant with salt—and the youngest daughter of a duke fell in love with each other at first sight.

Their first meeting happened when she had been riding a stallion, known to be exceptionally difficult to tame, around the field to appease him and almost ended up trampling the Crown Prince to death.

It would've been better if it just ended at that.

The day before he was to return to the imperial palace, in the evening where the sunset was particularly red. The duke's daughter had spent her whole life walking barefoot on the sandy beach with seagulls by the sea. She ran around in fields, picked fruits from trees along the street, and took naps on smooth warm rocks. On that day, she was proposed to by the Crown Prince.

While Freyja was sincerely overjoyed, she was also conflicted. The Crown Prince, however, told her to just trust him and proposed to take her into the imperial court. Freyja, who saw a flaming sunset that she'd never seen before inside his eyes, accepted his proposal.

Once the crown of the Crown Princess was placed on her head, the intelligent Freyja realized that she had walked into a cage on her own feet. And when she realized that her beloved person had been born and raised in the cage his whole life, she fell into despair.

At the imperial palace, Freyja was the most splendid flower in all high society. She talked, as she was told to, with the other nobles—instead of communing with the horses in the stable. She wasn't allowed to run and walk with hurried steps. She had to relearn how to walk to keep her stride and look elegant even in a hurry.

Instead of picking flowers in the field to make flower rings and crowns, she had to study expensive flowers that were difficult to name and even more difficult to grow. The empress had to learn how to perfectly arrange them into a favorable shape. Until the empress had accumulated enough knowledge and culture, she was also prohibited to read poetry and even to use her imagination to become a bird flying freely in the vast sky instead of the stuffy imperial palace.

Facing the thick philosophy book, Freyja grumbled that her head would turn as hard as rock if she continued to read it. The day she gifted a painting she had done to the emperor, he was so overjoyed that he put it into a frame and hung it in his chambers himself. However, the Empress Dowager had a hand in shoving that painting into the imperial treasure chest the very next day.

Even so, Freyja persevered through everything. She had her beloved husband by her side. Although he didn't have many ways to protect her as the Crown Prince, at least on days when the Crown Princess was severely reprimanded by the strict and harsh empress, he would hug her and give her space to cry.

Freyja, who soon became the empress, no longer remembered how to commune with the horses. It was also no longer possible for her to run down the long corridors of the palace in her heavy gowns. When she realized that she couldn't think of anything even when she read a poem, she fell into despair, shedding silent tears to maintain the dignity of an empress.

Eventually, she became used to living inside the cage.

"Isidore. When did you come?" A shadow was cast over the canvas. Freyja turned to offer him the beautiful smile that he had fallen in love with at first sight.

"It has been a while. My love, Freyja, what are you painting?"

Freyja adjusted her seat to make space for him to sit. The emperor wrinkled his forehead as he admired the painting as if he was going to give a strict evaluation. The sea made by generously using precious blue was so vivid he could almost feel the saltiness of each crashing white wave. In the middle of that sea, a boat sailed. As the emperor admired her ability to capture each person's characteristics so that they could be recognized by anyone even in a simple form, he looked at the painting even more closely.

"They look pretty familiar."

"Can you tell who is who?" The empress put down her brush and palette and took off her apron. She wrapped her arms around the emperor's neck and kissed his cheek.

The emperor embraced the empress and laid her down on the bed as he started to recite the names of the people in the painting one by one. They were the late parents of the empress, her siblings who had lost their lives young in an unfortunate accident, and even the previous empress who had been so difficult to deal with. There were no living members of the imperial family depicted there, but the emperor didn't notice it because he was too busy looking for peace and sanctuary in the empress' arms.

"What is the title of this painting?"

Freyja held out her hand to draw the curtains before answering. "*Freedom*."

Leonhardt immediately ran into his chambers, took out his cypher, and reflected it in the mirror.

[■ Month ■ Day: Mother passed away.]

To think it would happen this year of all years! Leonhardt hid the cypher again just in case anyone could find it. He took gasping breaths. He couldn't let the incident that ruined his life—and perhaps Elizabeth's as well—happen again.

Empress Freyja Ivanna von Esphedor's official cause of death was drowning. When she visited her hometown for the first time in many years with the emperor, she lost her footing at the cliff by the shore and passed away just like that.

But Leonhardt knew the truth. At the time, his mother had been suffering from severe depression. His father bought all sorts of drugs to try to make her feel better, and he summoned jesters and minstrels with fascinating stories to the palace. But all of it was useless.

She wanted freedom. Although the emperor could give her everything, he couldn't give her that one thing.

Actually, he could. When Leonhardt came to him to question his mother's death, the emperor shouted and laughed like a madman in a drunk and half-abashed state. "I set Freyja free! From this tedious life! From the imperial family! She needed to die so she could be free from this cage! I granted her wish until the end, for her sake. Freyja, my love. Then who will set me free?"

A terrible shadow fell over the imperial court. The emperor vacillated between a state of normalcy and one of madness. Eventually, he committed himself to his chambers and remained secluded there, practically a dead man. As the

Crown Prince and his son, Leonhardt pleaded with the emperor to get himself together. He managed to avoid getting deposed as the Crown Prince and ended up being confined in his own chambers.

While the imperial family was in turmoil, a flock of crows and rats in the shape of humans began to flock to the palace. And in their center was the duke of Elysium.

It will definitely not end up like that this time. Elysium will collapse just like this. I don't want to see father turning into a figurehead like before.

When Leonhardt ridiculed the emperor, saying he should have followed his mother in death, his father merely smiled and agreed, lamenting the constrained life of an emperor who couldn't even die as he wished. Even after inheriting the throne, Leonhardt had to revive the nation that had collapsed domestically and restore the international diplomatic relations that had completely turned.

If I have to go through that awful crap, I'd rather bite my tongue and die. Wait... Leonhardt let out a deep sigh, his forehead on the desk, when a sharp pain made him jolt upright.

What did Elizabeth do all that time?

He and Ilysses had been working so hard to revive the ruined nation that they put temporary beds inside the office and slept there. There was no way that the empress didn't do anything in the meantime.

Come to think of it, the domestic state of affairs unexpectedly calmed down without any riot happening... Leonhardt tried to reach out a little further into that memory.

Elizabeth was at a spot almost out of reach. He remembered getting the report that the empress personally went out of the palace to calm the angry mob. Even if she was hit by rotten vegetables or eggs chucked from the crowd, she kept smiling as she distributed her private property to the people.

Leonhardt smiled as he sat further upright. And then in a solemn manner, he slammed his head against the desk with so much force as if he wanted to break the desk.

It is impossible to be loved by everyone. There was nothing that could turn into a severe hatred more easily than a light affection. It was normal for someone to feel like they didn't even want to see the other person breathe once they felt any hint of hatred. Moreover, as much as people had a little bit of fantasy and good feelings when they heard the empress' name, it was just as easy to show blatant resentment towards her.

The empress had to endure that by herself. She never showed that she was having a hard time. Rather, she worried about his health, replaced the flowers in the study, and used that as a consolation to persevere and endure.

Otherwise, she might as well have erased her true self while repeatedly saying "perfect empress," beating herself up continuously in her journal. No, she was like that, too, in real life. Leonhardt sent away the servants who had gathered after hearing the loud noise from the Crown Prince's chambers. He headed to the bath. In the washroom, he filled the sink with cold water and slammed his forehead again on the icy surface. When he made a splash and dipped his face, the cold pierced the top of his head into his swelling forehead and caused him to scream.

"Blplplplplp…" Of course, it was only a floundering sound at best beneath the water. Still, Leonhardt shouted and screamed.

And then he made a vow. This time, he would never ever allow such a tragedy to happen. Mother might be looking like she was having fun and laughing happily nowadays, but if he thought about the conversation he had had with Mimis Brunnr, he couldn't afford to be complacent.

"Pwah…!" Leonhardt straightened after hitting his limit. He glared into the mirror. The bright golden hair he had inherited from his mother was soaked, streaked like golden leaves covered in autumn frost.

I will... I will definitely stop the same tragedy from happening... I have to... That's how... that's how Lizzie will become happy.

If mother hadn't died and father hadn't become an invalid... if he himself didn't inherit the throne at a young age and have to immediately jump into the political scene with nothing on his back... and if the empress hadn't had to endure everything alone with no place to rely on...

Everything is for the empress' happiness.

Maybe... Elizabeth could've lived a little happier.

THIRTY-FIVE

"Leon?"

It was Elizabeth. As Leonhardt staggered away from the bathroom, roughly wiping his wet hair, he bumped into her.

"What happened? The maids ran out to get a doctor just now. Did you get hurt?"

"Elizabeth."

"Y-yes?" Elizabeth was startled for a moment by Leonhardt calling her name in such an exhausted voice. She was still too young to read the emotion swirling behind his messy hair that was just wiped roughly with a towel and his cold eyes. So instead of assuming his feelings, she focused more on the ticklish sensation in a corner of her heart.

His shining golden hair and eyes that held violets, along with his thick eyelashes that looked like a wheat field on an autumn day, his gracefully bent nose bridge under the light, and his soft lips that always spoke gentle words, mesmerized her. If the white haired, red-eyed boy earlier was like a rabbit, then Leonhardt looked like a lion, just as his name suggested. He might be a lion who was only beginning to grow a mane, but his devotion and tendency to give all good things to his fiancée had spread throughout the imperial palace by word of mouth among the maids.

It wasn't just throughout the imperial palace. All of high society had been talking about Leonhardt and Elizabeth tirelessly. Especially since both of them were growing into adolescence, the story of their love affair had always been the perfect topic for those who were starving for an interesting anecdote. Stories about those two, sweet as sugar, were probably being told back and forth between the noble wives' fans at a tea party held by one of them even right now.

However, the reality was different from the rumors going around that Lady Elizabeth most likely also felt a very deep affection for His Highness and that she dreamed of him every night. In truth, she didn't even know what feelings swirled around in her heart, and she didn't understand why a little corner in her heart would feel ticklish and her face would burn up whenever she saw him looking like that. Though at the very least, she knew how much Leonhardt worried for her—just like the rumors that "His Highness takes such good care of the lady."

"Are you okay...?"

Am I okay? Leonhardt pulled up his face muscles that had been caving in. He wished for her to always act freely, with a smile on her face, and only want to say sweet and pleasant things. Yet he had made Elizabeth, the person he wanted so much to make happy, worry about him again. "Sorry... I'm sorry, Elizabeth..."

"Sorry? For what? What's wrong with you suddenly? Did you really get hurt? Did you smash your head on something again? I told you to stop doing that! Your head will go bad."

"Maybe I've really become stupid, as you say. The notorious moron! Dunce! Foolish jerk!"

"L-Leon...?"

Leonhardt pulled Elizabeth into a hug. He wanted to make her happy, but there was absolutely nothing he could give her as a nineteen-year-old young Crown Prince.

Elizabeth just blinked and she carefully raised her hand to start patting Leonhardt's back. She consulted Mimir about Leonhardt's weird tendency to suddenly hit his head against the wall or table in the middle of a conversation, and Mimir had replied nonchalantly, continuing to stir with an oversized spoon.

'He's in puberty. If you let him be, he's going to kick his blanket in the middle of the night later so just leave him alone.'

'Still... is there nothing I can do for Leon?'

'You're such a saint. Just what do you like about His Highness that you keep on talking about Leon, Leon? Even if you're already betrothed...'

'Obviously, it's because Leon is cool! He always treats me gently! He's kind, and… makes me have fun…'

'Kids these days are so precocious. If His Highness does that again, just pat his back and coax him by saying oh dear, good boy, coochy-coochy-coo.'

'Coochy-coochy-coo? Is that a magic spell?'

'Yes. It's a spell with a very high efficacy, so use it in a place with a lot of people next time. Don't forget to tell me how it goes.'

It seemed like this was the right time to use that magic.

"Oh dear, good boy, our Crown Prince Leonhardt. Coochy-coochy-coo."

Leonhardt doubted his ears for a moment. What did she just say?

"Good boy, good boy. What are you sorry for, Leon? Did you eat something tasty by yourself without me knowing? But it's okay. Leon needs to quickly grow bigger than you are now."

"…Lizzie…" In his young fiancée's arms, Leonhardt could feel the complicated thoughts and the tension that had been weighing down his shoulders vanish in an instant.

Seeing Leonhardt's complicated face mixed with half relief, half dejection, and a little astonishment, Elizabeth was in awe of the effectiveness of the spell Mimir taught her.

"Seems like Mimir taught you something weird again... but I'm okay. I didn't eat anything without you knowing, and..."

"Even though your forehead is this red?"

"...I just slipped when I was dozing off in front of the desk."

When Elizabeth brushed up Leonhardt's bangs, she furrowed her eyebrows and made a sad face as if she had been the one who was hurt.

Seeing that, Leonhardt felt his heart twinge again. *Don't make that face and please smile, Lizzie. Don't worry about someone like me...*

"Didn't you have something to do?"

"What can I even do when I usually just eat and play around in the imperial palace...? Unlike a certain His Highness, I've done all of my homework, you know?"

"Oh right, homework... Can't you just show me your homework?"

Elizabeth put on the most terrifying look she could muster. Leonhardt waved his hand to pretend to be scared, even though Elizabeth looked so awfully adorable with her puffed cheeks and frown. "No, no, no. I'll do it with my own abilities. I can do it. I have to do my own thing, do my own thing..."

"I'm really going to be angry if you do that again."

But Leonhardt had never seen Elizabeth actually get angry. Leonhardt was enjoying her harmless threat when he suddenly realized that he was still in Elizabeth's arms. He separated himself from her. There was a dark, round water stain that had dropped from his hair onto Elizabeth's shoulder.

"Sorry. Your clothes are soaked. Oh, should I introduce you to that Ils? That, uh... rabbit-like boy who's white, red, and carrying a big book."

"I think he's going to take a while since he went to meet Master Mimis Brunnr..."

"Then want to stroll around the rose garden?"

"Umm... I don't want to walk anymore today."

"Then..."

"I want to take a nap. Let me use your bed," Elizabeth said with a cheerful smile, feeling relieved to see Leonhardt return to his usual self. She had gone walking in the rose garden, looked around the palace, and admired the knights' swordsmanship training, so she wanted to do something she hadn't tried before this time.

"What's wrong with your bed?"

"Bailey's sleeping on it."

"Again?" Leonhardt couldn't bear to be jealous of his beloved companion dog, so he could only pull on his damp hair as if he was squeezing out the water from it. "I... I see... Have a nice sleep... I'm going to do my homework, so don't mind me..." Small round water droplets dripped on the floor as he walked away toward his desk and to actually start his homework.

Elizabeth watched Leonhardt walk away before she got up. "I'm leaving."

"Oh? Oh... okay..."

"I said I'm leaving."

"Huh? S-sure. Bye...?"

"You're not going to stop it?"

Stop? Stop what? Stop talking? Leonhardt stared at Elizabeth. For some reason, Elizabeth had a very displeased and disappointed look of dissatisfaction on her face. Leonhardt felt his heart fall that instant. He didn't know what it was, but he felt like he had made a huge mistake.

Should I go to Mimir in the Clock Tower and ask her to turn back time now...?

"Wh-why would I stop you...? Lizzie, you can do anything you want. You have my permission. Do whatever you want. It is my room, but you can enter it anytime you want, and leave it anytime you want as well. My bed? You can use my bed anytime. So..."

"Your Highness... is a-an idiot!" Elizabeth shut her eyes tightly as she uttered words that could amount to treason. With a stomp, she turned around and darted back to her own chambers—which was basically the room right across Leonhardt's.

Leonhardt was left alone and bewildered, water still dripping from his hair. Why was Elizabeth acting that way?

Don't tell me... don't tell me Lizzie is going through puberty too? That sweet and kind Lizzie? No way would Lizzie run away from home, mess up her room because she doesn't like it, and flip a dining table upside down, right? Leonhardt worried, remembering all the acts of brutality he had committed the first time he had gone through puberty.

Elizabeth cried until her shoulders shook. She clung to Bailey. Lately, she had been having a hard time controlling her emotions. Every time she saw Leonhardt, her heart raced so rapidly it ached. Then she would get cranky because of that strange sensation she couldn't get used to and ended up wanting to tease or bother him. But at the same time, she also hated to see him get hurt because of her words.

What was she supposed to do? Leonhardt didn't know about it, but the maids of the Crown Prince's palace who were in charge of her all knew. They said that puberty finally came for Elizabeth, so she started to have an affection for His Highness the Crown Prince.

Everyone says that it'll be okay, and that everyone goes through this at my age... but... but still... What if Leonhardt got disappointed in her behavior and said that he wanted to call their betrothal off? She didn't even want to imagine it. Elizabeth cried loudly, still holding tightly to Bailey as she asked him, "Do I also look that strange to you?"

"Woof?"

"...Forget it. I can't even talk about this to a human, how can I do it to a dog?"

Sniffle...

Bailey was much smarter than the average canine, but he was unfortunately not wise enough to understand his owner's psychological state during puberty. Bailey whined, wondering why his master was making such a sad face, and circled around Elizabeth before bringing over his favorite toy.

I'll give this to master so she will feel better.

However, when Elizabeth looked at Bailey smiling and panting with his tongue half stuck out, her expression became even sadder, and she started weeping again.

Are you hurt? Did something happen to master? Is someone hurting master? Bailey stood upright. If he stood on both feet and leaned on her, she would lie down on the floor and pretend she was defeated. Then she would laugh along with him as they rolled around on the floor.

But instead of lying down on the floor, she started to wail as she held onto Bailey. Bailey licked off the salty tears flowing down Elizabeth's cheek and smelled the scent coming out from her embrace. He didn't know exactly what happened, but the young man who was always with his owner was the one who made her like this. He resolved to bite off the man's shoes the next time they met. Bailey shook a little to make more space for Elizabeth to bury her face in his soft fur.

CHAPTER
THIRTY-SIX

Leonhardt carefully pressed his ear against Elizabeth's closed door. He could hear sobbing and Bailey whimpering.

Lizzie... is crying because of me again...? Leonhardt staggered backward and hit the back of his head against the wall. *What should I do? The ways to soothe a girl going through puberty are not written in any book!*

Leonhardt paced back and forth. How could he make Elizabeth smile again?

Should I invite her to play somewhere? No, she said that she doesn't want to walk anymore today. Today? If she says she doesn't want to walk today, will she want to tomorrow? Go out? Going out... Hm... Hmm... Hmmm... That's it! Leonhardt flicked his fingers in the air. He had come up with something that might be able to prevent his mother's tragedy from happening, let Elizabeth experience something new, and just make everyone smile.

"Lizzie...? Can I come in...?"

"Don't... come...! *Hic...*"

"Okay..." He hesitated. "Then can I talk from over here...?"

"Aren't you the one who can do anything you want yourself, Your Highness? Before you tell me to do as I like, anything is fine, or do whatever I want, how about Your Highness show some examples first?!"

Even Elizabeth herself knew that there was no logic in what she just said. But as if she were under a bad magic spell, she kept saying things that would provoke other people. Elizabeth covered her mouth with her hand as she sniffled through her nose. If she opened her mouth anymore, she was afraid that she would really say something bad.

Seems like it is puberty... Leonhardt smiled bitterly as he let out a sigh. It would be okay. At least she wasn't flipping the table or asking for a tree to be cut because she didn't want to see leaves falling...

That tree! Leonhardt apologized to the innocent tree. The biggest tree with the widest branches in the Crown Prince's garden nodded the tip of its branch in the summer wind, as if it were accepting his apology.

But I'm glad that Lizzie can express her aversion towards something... Wait, no! Not at all! She shouldn't be doing it like this, but something more... More... I mean, she shouldn't be averse to me but something else, you dumb Leonhardt! No... Honestly, I hope Lizzie would always think positively of me... But that's just your greed in the end, so just focus on comforting Lizzie, you fool!

As Leonhardt leaned the top of his head against the marble wall and reprimanded himself severely, he cleared his throat. Being rejected by Lizzie hurt his heart more than the pain in his head after hitting his forehead, back of his head, and top of his head against something. He said, "Then I'll act freely like you said. Lizzie, do you want to go see the sea? No. This is an order. Lady Elizabeth, go to the sea with me."

A long pause in which the sobs quieted. And then, "The sea?" It took some time, but Elizabeth finally opened the door and showed herself, her nose strawberry-red. At her feet, Bailey growled and bared his teeth.

Leonhardt lifted an eyebrow at Bailey. Why was looking at him like that? Bailey leaned forward to grab the shoes of the bad person who made his owner cry. Elizabeth tried to stop Bailey. However, Bailey didn't understand why his owner would do that, and he sunk his teeth in, nipping the foot beneath the shoe. Leonhardt shook him off gently and returned to the conversation, asking, "Have you ever seen it?"

"No..." Elizabeth had only ever lived in the Elysium residence or the imperial palace all her life, so she shook her head. She knew what a sea was thanks to the books that she read. At the very least, she understood the role it played in nature so well that her teacher was impressed. But she'd never seen it with her own eyes.

Whenever the sea was mentioned, it was always accompanied by how large it was or how the end couldn't be seen over the horizon. Elizabeth felt curious about that, so she opened her door a little wider for Leonhardt to come in through.

"You know that my mother came from a place with a seaside port, right?"

"Yes, Your Highness. I know that it is called the empire's best vacation spot."

"Just talk to me comfortably."

"Is that also an order, Your Highness?"

"Are you going to keep acting so formal?"

"You told me to do whatever I want, Your Highness."

"Do what you like," he replied. "Anyway, it's almost summer, and that place always holds a drama festival in summer."

"A drama festival?"

"It's a theatrical play with the legend passed down in mother's hometown as the basis. It's always the same plot, but it's interesting to see how it gets newly interpreted and directed every year. I thought that it would be great if you watch it... and... umm..."

Elizabeth tilted her head.

"Father fell in love with mother at first sight at that place, you see," Leonhardt blurted, his eyes scrunched closed. It was the perfect place to make the heart of a seventeen-year-old girl flutter, a girl who was in her puberty and might be dreaming of a prince charming on a white horse.

I feel a bit bad for basically selling father out... but please let me off since this is all for the sake of everything going well! Leonhardt secretly asked for forgiveness from the emperor, who was taking a nap in the empress' chambers. He continued to Elizabeth, "You've never gone to the sea, right? And the play that will appear on the last day of the festival will be good for your artistic value, culture studies, and other education..."

"I want to go!"

All right! Leonhardt shouted in delight inside. Elizabeth's eyes that looked cold just now returned to looking like doe eyes. After Leonhardt confirmed the curiosity, excitement, and expectation lighting up her features, he held out his arm as if he was going to escort Elizabeth.

"Before that, I have to go somewhere first. Will you accompany me?"

"Certainly!" Elizabeth grinned again as she rested her hand on Leonhardt's arm.

"I want to go to the sea."

Hearing the empress' words made the emperor's thick eyebrows twitch.

"The sea... the sea is good. But Freyja, I think that my love, which is wider than the ocean, would be better than the sea..."

"The ocean is endless. When I was little, I would wonder what would be beyond the horizon as I looked at it."

"I think, my love... Ah, Freyja. Did I perhaps do something wrong again?" the emperor asked, worried. He straightened his back and placed both of his hands on the empress' shoulders, locking her in his embrace.

The empress' gaze was far off and hazy, as if she were daydreaming. She said, "Now I know that there's another kingdom on the other side beyond the horizon, but... the day I first met Your Majesty, I was riding on a horse to run towards the horizon to find out what's beyond there. Do you remember?"

"If you're talking about that time I was taking a nap after sneaking away from my mother and the maids and almost got my head crushed by that horse's hooves, I wouldn't be able to forget that even if I wanted to." The emperor muttered, leaning gently into the empress' embrace, and laying his head on her.

"I want to go to the sea. I want to see the waves. I want to hear the seagulls sing instead of the tedious and boring music the palace orchestra plays. Your Majesty. Please?"

"Freyja..." The emperor straightened his body again, frowning. There was no reason to reject her request. He had excellent ministers whom he could trust to govern for a while, and it was nearly summer, and...

"Your Majesty, His Highness the Crown Prince and Lady Elizabeth are requesting an audience."

Upon hearing this, the emperor and the empress scurried to find their clothes, each wondering whom the audience request was specifically for. "This isn't fair. My love only needs to wear a dress and a shawl, while I have to put on a shirt, then a pair of pants, and then..."

"Then I should give Your Majesty the pajamas I wear."

"Freyja!"

After hearing that the children had come, the empress' face turned bright again, as if it was always that way.

"Does asking for an audience usually take this long?"

"Umm... I think we came at the wrong time."

"Wrong time?"

"You know."

Elizabeth and Leonhardt were crouched down in front of the bedroom in the empress' palace, resting their chins on their hands and staring at the servant. The servant was sweating a bunch, not knowing how to explain what was happening inside, trying to buy some time.

"Let them in." With the emperor's deep, dignified voice, the bedroom door opened.

Leonhardt entered his mother's room with Elizabeth's hand in his, in a manner befitting a prince. *That painting...*

The ocean. A vast blue ocean with no end in sight and a small boat tossed gently on the waves. But the people on the boat were all already dead and free from everything. Leonhardt, who knew what meaning it held, bit his lower lip, and immediately got straight to the point. "Father, mother, I have a request."

"Daughter-in-law, you've gotten so much prettier! Do you have anything you want? Do you want to learn how to paint with the empress? If it were for you, I'd even get diamonds ground to mix into the paint instead of a lapis lazuli!"

"Father..."

"Oh, right, you're here. Do you have a request? For now, let us hear it."

Leonhardt took a deep breath. For a moment, he thought that it would've been great if he had a little sister who could get all the love his father was showing to his daughter-in-law. He said, "We want to see the sea."

"What? No."

"Let us go!"

"Freyja!" The emperor had been going to disregard the Crown Prince's words, but he quickly cried out the empress' name when she chimed in. Meanwhile, Elizabeth managed to get out of the emperor's embrace and returned to Leonhardt's side.

"Freyja, I can do everything for your sake. But..."

"The children are here. Let us not discuss this any further. My sweethearts, why do you suddenly want to see the sea?"

Leonhardt and Elizabeth exchanged glances. Elizabeth then opened her mouth with her heart full of palpitating expectation. "I would like to see the drama festival held in Her Majesty's hometown. Because... because I've never seen the sea... and it is now summer, and His Highness suggested it first."

"The Crown Prince did? How admirable. Your Majesty, how about we take this chance to have a vacation as a family?"

"What a great idea! My love, Freyja."

Leonhardt pouted internally, frustrated with his father.

"Does Your Majesty hate the sea?" Elizabeth, after getting the empress' permission, studied the paint and nearby brush. She noticed the emperor looking doubtful.

The emperor hesitated, but, after a moment said, "I do not hate it."

"His Highness said... umm... that it was the place where you two first met... that is what makes me want to go see it, too."

"The Crown Prince did? Freyja, have you ever told how our first meeting went to that boy Leon?"

"No...? Then did Your Majesty...?"

The emperor shook his head as he blinked his eyes.

Leonhardt bit his tongue, feeling himself break out in cold sweat. Come to think of it, he heard about how their first meeting went when the emperor, who had become an invalid, was rambling in his drunken state.

"N-now that I think about it, we've never gone out together after Lizzie came to the palace! So please grant us your permission, Your Majesty." Leonhardt changed the subject in a hurry.

The emperor and the empress stared at him a bit suspiciously, but then they exchanged glances with each other.

"We shall go. As it happens, the empress was also just talking about the sea." The emperor nodded.

But Leonhardt couldn't feel overjoyed at the permission that he unexpectedly granted. "Mother, too?" Leonhardt felt his heart sink again. He had a feeling that everything would go wrong.

"At this time of the year, they would be installing a stage on the beach, and I would run within the vicinity of the stage with my older brothers... I can't believe I will be able to see that again! Let us hurry and get ready."

When a cactus felt rain after a long drought, a flower grew—one as beautiful as the time it had to endure its thirst. The empress' smile was reminiscent of that. Although Leonhardt still couldn't get rid of his uneasiness, he played along with Elizabeth, who was so happy she seemed like she would jump.

HAND AND HAND, EYE AND EYE

CHAPTER
THIRTY-SEVEN

During their sword training, after hearing that the entire imperial family would be going on a vacation together to the sea, Albert spoke up as he parried Leonhardt's sword. "Oh... that place... I see... I also went there for my honeymoon. It was very beautiful."

"Your wife was? Or the sea?"

"My wife with her bright smile as she was looking at the sea... No, that's not it. Your Highness!"

"Should I get your wife a local specialty as a souvenir?"

"I would be grateful, but anyway, why do you look so downcast even though you're going to such a nice place?"

Leonhardt pierced through Albert's defense with a sharp move, as if he had already predicted it. As Albert had expected and predicted, Leonhardt grew so much that it was like he was already skilled with sword since he was born. Now, he was too much to handle by himself.

"By the way, did you hear anything about the drama festival?"

"Oh, I happened to have the catalog with me. If I had time... Oh dear. I was going to go... Phew... But it is what it is."

"Sir Bern, you're going to be in trouble if you don't focus."

"Your Highness is the one making me not focus!" Albert let the attack pass with a simple move to the side before moving behind Leonhardt's back and twisting his arm. It was close, but victory once again went to Albert.

"Show me that catalog," Leonhardt turned his stiff shoulder around and said to Albert.

Albert took out a particularly colorful paper among the documents resting on his work desk.

"The Little Mermaid, who realized that she would never get what she wanted by the prince's side, turned into bubbles and gained true freedom...?" Leonhardt wondered aloud.

"That's how they're interpreting it this time," Albert said. "Well, compared to the last year when they made the prince a nutcase who cut a woman's tendons and poisons her so he can make her his nameless concubine, isn't this much saner content?"

"So even such an interpretation could make it on stage."

"Thanks to that, it became a topic of heated debate among the critics for some time."

"Thanks for the information. I'll see you after my vacation," Leonhardt said.

"Oh, Your Highness. Uh... with all due respect, would you mind if I were to ask you for a favor?"

"What is it?" Leonhardt was about to hurry out because Elizabeth was waiting for him outside the training ground, but Albert held him back urgently.

The man who was two heads taller than most was staring sentimentally into the distance, his cheeks flushed. "Umm... if you go... can you get me a long seaweed..."

Seaweed? Leonhardt wondered, puzzled by the request. *He hadn't even been married for a month, so why... Don't tell me? His wife is...* Leonhardt's eyes widened as he said, "Albert, don't tell me you..."

"Ahem, ahem! Ahem, ahem! Ahem!"

Leonhardt shook his head, momentarily feeling like there was no one he could trust.

Seeing him walk in quick steps to leave the training ground, Albert shouted, "The best one! You have to get the best one! Your Highness! Okay? Are you listening? Your Highness!"

"Something smells strange," Elizabeth said when she opened the window and basked in the sea breeze.

Hearing that, the empress moved closer to the carriage window and held out her hand outside. The wind brushing against her hand was laden with salt. "It's the smell of the sea!"

"The smell of the sea?"

"This unique salty and damp wind, along with the fishy smell of seaweed. I'm really back in my hometown!" the empress said, beaming along with Elizabeth. Leonhardt and the emperor had similar smiles as they watched their beloved ladies.

"I can see white birds there! Is that a seagull?"

"That's right. I'll show you something fun once we get a little closer to the sea."

"Something fun...?"

The empress settled back in her seat despite looking like she wanted to jump out of the carriage at once. The closer they got to the sea, the more the old memories that the empress had to erase from her heart by force were coming out one by one. Memories of riding a horse through the sea breeze, lying on a black stone on the beach and basking in the warm sun. Memories of sitting alone on the sand and tearing up at the sound of waves the night before she had to leave her hometown.

"I thought I would never be able to hear this again..." she muttered.

The emperor's and Leonhardt's gazes were directed at the empress.

The empress spoke in disbelief as she looked at the distant horizon in a daze, "To think I would be able to hear the song of the seas again. This dream won't suddenly stop, will it?"

Although the territory that was the empress' hometown had to be returned to the imperial court because there was no one to inherit the title, the subjects living there were proud of the fact that it was the best vacation spot in the empire. The officials who came from the imperial court let the subjects do whatever they wanted under the emperor's order, as long as they didn't cross the line. They were even granted autonomy and allowed to form an association. That was how they made the hometown that the empress loved even more beautiful.

When the empress arrived at the mansion that had become the imperial family's summer villa, she greeted the old servants who still managed the mansion. She hadn't seen them for such a long time. Watching the empress, the emperor regretted that he hadn't come here with her earlier.

Leonhardt watched his father and resolved not to be like him. *Wait, wouldn't letting Lizzie return to her hometown mean*

I would be returning her to that wretched duke of Elysium's residence? No, no, I take it back. I take that resolution back.

"Leon? What's wrong?"

"Lizzie, how about making this your second hometown?"

"Huh?"

While the servants were organizing their luggage, the imperial family members went to look around the beach. Elizabeth wore a light, white linen sundress with a puffy three-tiered skirt. Over it, she wore a loosely tied lace bolero to prevent sunburn, and a pair of exotic sandals with jewels and knot ornaments. With her hair tied in pigtails and covered with a straw hat, she was ready for her first time at the beach.

The empress appeared in front of the emperor wearing the most natural and comfortable dress she could wear as the empress.

"You could've worn your old clothing since we came to your hometown for the first time in a while."

"Unfortunately, the size doesn't match anymore. Seems like I've been living too well in the imperial court."

Leonhardt wore a white shirt that would reveal his silhouette when the wind blew, along with black trousers. He had a subtle-looking sword on his waist and a headscarf on his head like a sailor. He held his hand out. "Then, shall we go, Lady Elizabeth?"

When they arrived at the beach, the empress stretched her arms up in the air clutching fresh, hot french fries. Just then, a seagull snatched the fries from her hand in one nimble swoop.

"Oh my God!"

"See, wasn't it fun?"

Elizabeth's eyes widened as she covered her gaping mouth with her hands. The empress then began to scatter the fries high up in the sky. Elizabeth was only watching her at first, but she gathered her courage and lifted some fries in her hand as well. Something swooped down and grabbed them from her grasp.

"Oh my gosh..." Elizabeth took more fries and scattered them in the air like the empress.

Unlike the emperor, who watched white seagulls squawk around the empress and Elizabeth with amusement, Leonhardt was lost in serious thought. *I think the ending of the play in the drama festival needs to be changed... but will they listen to me?*

As the emperor drank a cool fruit juice, he glanced at his son. Leonhardt's expression looked as if he just heard that the world was ending. The emperor prompted, "Do you have something on your mind?"

"Father... that... umm... it's nothing."

"Tell me. It doesn't come very often when we get to have an enjoyable time. It's unforgivable by the imperial order that only you would make such a face."

Is father making a joke right now? Leonhardt looked up at the emperor in disbelief. After opening and closing his mouth a few times, he finally spoke up. He really needed the emperor's help this time. "About mother's painting."

"Ah... you mean that painting she titled '*Freedom*.' What's wrong with it?"

"The sea has always represented freedom. The sea is mother's hometown, and I've heard what kind of person mother was before she met you. So, if she missed the sea... Oh dang it!" Leonhardt threw up his hands. "Father, have you noticed?"

"Wh-what are you talking about?"

Leonhardt, who had been trying to give an in-depth explanation about the sea and freedom, judged that he wouldn't get to the point until the sun set at this rate. He inhaled slowly and tried again, "How many people on that boat are still alive?"

"Hoo, you little?" Realization crossed the emperor's face. He looked at his son proudly.

"Isn't it concerning?"

"Now that you say it, it is very concerning."

"However, of all things, the ending of the drama festival this year is 'The Little Mermaid' with her realizing that her true wish is freedom then turning into bubbles as a result."

"You little! How can you spoil the ending suddenly... What did you say?"

"Isn't it concerning?"

"Extremely concerning indeed. And then?"

"I'm thinking of getting used to abusing my power with you as my example, father."

"We need to respect the intention of artists. But..."

"It's concerning, isn't it?" Leonhardt grinned as he observed the emperor's reaction. There was no way his father, of all people, didn't understand what he was saying.

"I shall not be in your way, Crown Prince. However, I shall not back you either."

"Thank you, father." After receiving what seemed like a noncommittal permission from the emperor, Leonhardt called Elizabeth over, and they headed to the outdoor stage set up on the sandy beach.

"Where's Avon?"

The workers who were busy moving around because the drama festival was already around the corner all stopped moving. However, none of them knew the young man who was looking for the person in charge of the drama festival.

Leonhardt ended up having to reveal his identity to a worker who was on a break. The worker was so surprised and felt the need to tell his supervisor, who told his own supervisor, who also told his supervisor, of the Crown Prince and his fiancée's visit.

"Y-Your Highness the Crown Prince! What are you all doing?! Hurry and pay your respects!"

"Who's looking for m... Oh my, what an honorable guest we have here."

Elizabeth hid behind Leonhardt's back, as was her habit whenever she faced a stranger. Avon, who appeared while scratching his disheveled spiky hair, was the director and playwright.

"I want you to change the ending," Leonhardt announced.

Avon, who had fallen asleep while writing the script yesterday to the point that one side of his face was smudged with print, twitched his eyebrow. "...Everyone, out."

"A-Avon!"

"I said get out!"

Leonhardt frowned at Avon's attitude. Maybe all artists were crazy. After the two, no, three of them were left inside, Avon slumped onto a chair, ready to talk it out.

"Just change the ending. Avon, your interpretation is outstanding. However... I want my fiancée and mother to shed tears of joy and happiness rather than one of sadness and sorrow."

"What about a touching feeling?"

"Isn't that a given?"

Avon grinned at Leonhardt's words. The Crown Prince in front of him was abusing his power to rudely invade an artist's creative territory. Moreover, he was using the fiancée hiding behind him and the empress as an excuse. "Then, Your Highness has another ending in mind?"

Leonhardt was conflicted. The ending that he was going to talk about was an ending that Avon was going to write in a few years to come. "...That prince, does he really need to be the king?"

"It isn't even mentioned in the original version, so it wouldn't matter if the prince isn't the king."

"Then it wouldn't matter if he becomes a sailor, right?"

"A sailor?" Avon sat up.

A prince that doesn't become a king, a prince that gives up on the throne by himself, a prince that loses the battle for the throne, among other things. Brilliant ideas zipped around his head.

As Leonhardt watched Avon rushing to find a pen and ink, he asked for the future Avon's understanding in his heart. "How about making the ending be the prince becoming a sailor and the Little Mermaid staying by his side as a mermaid, and they go on a voyage together forever more?"

Avon moved his pen on paper frantically like a machine. Then he stopped. As he kept on muttering the three words sailor, mermaid, and voyage over and over again, he started to rip apart the completed script.

"A-Avon?"

"This is an abuse of power. An abuse, I say! How could you give me this idea with only a week left until the performance?!"

"I believe in your talent."

"Just lay a curse on me instead!" Avon retorted, caught between laughing and crying.

Leonhardt smiled, proud of the result, as he and Elizabeth took their leave.

"...Will it really be okay?"

"I'm a little sorry to them, but both me and father wouldn't want our beloved life companion to cry in sadness, even though it's just a drama."

Beloved life companion? In an instant, Elizabeth's face turned beet red, and it was as if steam were rising from her head.

Avon, alone, kept muttering the final words the Crown Prince had whispered to his ear. "If one wants to keep their beloved bird inside a cage, then he should at least have the courage and determination to make the whole world its cage."

Birdcage, birds, just what did the lady who grew up freely by the sea go through in the imperial court? That was the moment before a surge of ideas started to burst inside Avon's head.

"How does the story of 'The Little Mermaid' originally go?"

"Wait, you didn't know, Lizzie?"

"Mother used to tell me that such a fairytale is not suitable for an empress," Elizabeth said with a small voice as she looked up at the sky.

Leonhardt gritted his teeth and resented the duchess of Elysium once again. He started to tell Elizabeth the story of "The Little Mermaid" in a clumsy way as they walked.

"So, it was actually such a sad story..." she said after he told her.

"Everyone has been putting out their reinterpretation of it, though. Don't you think it's better for a fairy tale to end happily ever after?"

"Is that so? But Leon..." Elizabeth stopped walking.

With a dubious expression, Leonhardt also stopped and looked around.

"...where are we?"

They had been so preoccupied with their talk that Elizabeth and Leonhardt had ended up on a road far from the beach. Elizabeth glanced around at the unfamiliar place and hugged Leonhardt's arm tightly, scooting closer to him.

Leonhardt was wondering what he should do in this unfamiliar yet also familiar place. It was that time of the year, so the biggest street was restricted to carriages. Moreover, street stalls were starting to be built alongside the edges.

We won't be able to get back by carriage like this...

After a short moment of conflict, Leonhardt clicked his tongue and called over a boy who was looking around for work. He told him, "Go to the villa owned by the imperial family... I mean, go to that mansion over there and tell His Majesty the Emperor that the Crown Prince and Lady Elizabeth will be coming back late. If you show this, no one will doubt you. Enjoy the festival with this money." Leonhardt took off the bandana he had been wearing and gave it to the boy along with a few gold coins he took out from his pocket.

The boy looked at Leonhardt and the things in his hand alternatively with an expression of disbelief before bowing with determination and running towards the beach.

"Coming back late?" Elizabeth asked.

"The night market is going to open soon. Now that we're here, it won't be bad to see it before we leave."

Elizabeth nodded. She remembered the maids had once bragged with a smile about buying some cheap accessories at the night market. She was curious about what kind of place it was. "But will it be okay without any adults?"

"I'm here, aren't I? I'm going to be an adult soon. This sword right here is only for Lady Elizabeth... No, would it be better to call you Isolde for today?"

"Isolde?"

"No one knows who we are here, but it's just in case. For today, how about we become the common folks instead of a Crown Prince and a lady?"

Elizabeth contemplated this. "Then," she said, "Sir Tristan, I'll let you be my escort."

Still hearing the uneasiness in Elizabeth's voice, Leonhardt patted the back of her hand, as if telling her not to worry.

For some reason, her heart was fluttering. Was it because she kept hearing about the adventures of the pirates and sailors in the carriage? Elizabeth felt like she was going on an adventure like that.

As the sunset began to spread bright red flames along the slope, the lights hanging about, strung in the air like a clothesline, began to light one by one. It was a crude and shoddy decoration compared to the crystal chandelier that filled the large ballroom, but Elizabeth burst with joy.

"Shall we go now, Isolde?"

"Okay, Tristan!"

At least for the evening, both of them were not the Crown Prince Leonhardt and his fiancée, Elizabeth, but mere young lovers Isolde and Tristan. Elizabeth was amazed to see all kinds of accessories made from the sea sold by the street vendors.

"A clamshell only has one match in the whole world. It is often used as a charm for marital harmony and love of lovers, young miss."

"Really?"

As he showed a clamshell decoration filled with sparkling sand, a very small starfish, coral reef, and some seawater before being sealed with glass, the merchant then said, "Do you like it?"

"It's cute. I've never seen anything like this before."

"You can't get clamshells made into a glass bowl like this anywhere else but here. A while back, a very tall knight and his wife were also charmed by this and swept through all the displays."

"Le—Tristan... could that knight be..."

"A knight we know...?"

Leonhardt and Elizabeth—No, Tristan and Isolde exchanged looks at each other.

"Wait, do you guys know that knight? No wonder the clothes you're wearing looked spick and span. Okay! I'm in a good mood. I've raked in just enough thanks to that knight, so I'll give you guys these for cheap. Take one each." The merchant, who was able to guess the relationship between that knight and the little customers in front of him right away, said it as if he was being generous.

Even though Leonhardt knew that no merchant who said that would sell it cheaper than the regular price, he still decided to let it go this time. Elizabeth carefully picked a pair of clamshells but then picked another over and over again.

"Are you going with that? Good choice, they're as pretty as you, young lady and master." the merchant said, smiling.

The clamshells Elizabeth picked had a blue coral and a purple coral inside it. "Will you be able to make me happy until the day this sea all dries up?"

"If you want, I will do it forever even after the coral reefs withered." Leonhardt took Elizabeth's hand and kissed it. The shell bracelet the merchant had given to her for free made a pleasant clacking sound.

The farther they walked along the path, the stronger the smell of something delicious became. They paused before a stall that gave off a heavenly scent, where a steaming potato gleamed with a generous amount of butter and sparkled with salt, next to a skewered whole cob of grilled corn. Leonhardt and Elizabeth exchanged glances.

"What's that?" Elizabeth, who was looking around at the street food with excitement, had laid her eyes on something. While Leonhardt was deciding whether the roasted potato or the grilled corn would be tastier, his eyes went to what Elizabeth looked at. He froze at what he saw.

A stall selling whole grilled squid.

"That's a squid... The sailors call it the servants of Kraken or something. Anyway... umm... its texture is chewy, but still, isn't its shape quite something...?"

"I want to try eating that!"

"Li—no. Isolde?"

Elizabeth pestered Leonhardt with her sparkling eyes. That was the first time Elizabeth had ever seen food in that shape. One must always endure the risk when they go on an adventure. With the heart of a splendid adventurer, Elizabeth lightly shook Leonhardt's sleeve.

"...You might regret it."

Contrary to his worries, however, Elizabeth gladly took a bite, her eyes sparkling with curiosity.

"How is it?"

Elizabeth could only say her answer after a moment. Unlike the soft look on the grilled squid's exterior, she had to chew for quite a long time to swallow it. "It's chewy... and buttery... and... salty."

"Can you eat it all?"

Elizabeth nodded. With so many strange and interesting foods in front of her eyes, she couldn't even think about the food she was used to in the imperial palace like lobster or grilled shrimp.

"They're going to start the fireworks soon. Shall we have a seat somewhere while we eat?" Leonhardt suggested to Elizabeth after checking a poster in the plaza. Fireworks were something they could sometimes see from the imperial palace, but Leonhardt told Elizabeth that it would feel different to see the fireworks being shot up above the sea at night, when it would be so dark they wouldn't be able to tell ocean from darkness.

At the end, both of their hands were full of food as they climbed a hill that would have a good view of the fireworks. As it turned out, there were not many people around, and the night breeze was refreshingly cool. Serenaded by the sound of waves, the little spot felt cozy.

If only there weren't men in black following Leonhardt and Elizabeth. This place would've been the perfect place to make summer memories.

"Isolde, listen to me from now on."

"Huh? What's wrong, Tristan?"

Leonhardt drew the sword from his waist and stepped forward. Elizabeth realized what was going on and tensed up.

"Hey, stop hiding and come out. You might have ten fingers, but you have a lot more bones in your fingers, you know? I'll finish this before I crush every single one of them."

With Leonhardt's intimidation, the group of men that had been following them from inside the forest started to show themselves one by one.

Leonhardt grimaced at their rough, scowling faces. He said, "Just remember this. I'll let you know how many bones you have in your fingers if you dare to touch Isolde."

"Oh no, I'm so scared! Rather than such a nasty method, we, the Gentlemen of the Sea, prefer a much more refined way."

"Gentlemen of the Sea... are you pirates?"

"I said Gentlemen of the Sea! Now, young master. Look at this carefully." As he said that, the man held a sword in one hand and formed a fist in another hand. "This one's name is Conversation, and this one's name is Negotiation. Which one will you choose?"

Leonhardt took a deep sigh before saying to Elizabeth, "Isolde, close your eyes until I say you can open them. Okay?"

CHAPTER THIRTY-NINE

Elizabeth closed her eyes tightly. She had learned about what to do in case she encountered such an incident. But her mind went blank, and she couldn't think of anything. With her eyes closed, she heard not the disciplined shouts of knights at the training ground, but the sharp sounds of iron clashing against iron and shrill screams. Even if Leonhardt had improved his skills to the point that he could make the commander of the Imperial Order of Knights nervous, he was up against too many people.

As she wondered if it would be better to just reveal their identities, Elizabeth shook her head. Even if Leonhardt weren't a Crown Prince but the emperor, those men would probably still be happy to take them as hostages.

"I respect your determination to protect your lady, young master, so I shall give you a special show of the Gentlemen of the Sea's skills!"

Leonhardt clicked his tongue, wondering how these pirates could be called gentlemen. All of them rushed him at the same time, and he tightened his grip on his sword. He was at an absolute disadvantage. The moment he let his guard down, the thing that would flutter in the air wouldn't be the dazzling blond hair he inherited from his mother, but a part of his body.

But there was no choice. He had to win and show Elizabeth the fireworks over the night sea, which his mother loved. He needed to see Elizabeth's happiness. With that in mind, he charged and slashed his sword against the pirates' as if he was cutting the waves with a knife, avoiding their attacks by a nose.

"This young master... is pretty good?"

"Hah! He's still a greenhorn!"

Leonhardt gritted his teeth, watching for an opening and swinging his sword again. Leonhardt's sword skills were faithfully built from the basics in the imperial order. Compared to the rough and clumsy sword skills the pirates used to plunder, his were enough to overwhelm them.

Leonhardt doubted his own eyes. The pirates' movements looked strangely slow. At the same time, he felt an electrifying sensation on his fingertips along with a blue energy shaking like a haze over his sword. *This can't be...?*

Just to be sure, Leonhardt blocked the pirates' attack and countered again with his own. Everything was for Elizabeth's sake. He kept that in his mind, shaking off any other thoughts. Focus!

The blue energy radiated outward, growing stronger. Leonhardt didn't know whether to smile or cry as he thought, *I didn't know my awakening would be like this... Should I thank these guys?*

The pure energy rushed from his sword through his whole body, exhilarating him. He smirked, tightening his grip on his sword, and letting the energy overtake him.

It was just as written in the books. A sword master was really someone who had reached the peak of swordsmanship. Before he could think and judge with his mind, his body would already be moving to defend and attack in the most efficient way.

Leonhardt approached the pirates, who were falling to the ground one by one. He threatened, "So, who wants to know how many finger bones in your hands?"

Elizabeth, who suddenly couldn't hear a thing, felt terrified. *No way. There's no way Leon fell, right?* Anxiety thrummed in her heart so loud it drowned out all the other noises.

In the end, Elizabeth decided to try opening her eyes slightly. Leonhardt was one-sidedly playing around with the pirates with his sword. His expression radiated a fierce determination she'd never seen before. *Is that... really Leon...?*

His face was cold and resolute, like a divine being imposing retribution. Even to Elizabeth, who didn't know much about swordsmanship, he was obviously targeting the enemies' weak points without making any unnecessary movements.

She noticed one of the pirates, who was presumed to have passed out behind Leonhardt, rise to his feet again and carefully approach the Crown Prince. She wanted to shout at him to look behind, but she couldn't make a sound. In her frustration, tears streamed down her cheeks, and she stamped her feet.

However, Leonhardt managed to avoid the attack as if he had another set of eyes on his back. He grabbed the enemy in front of him by the collar and threw him backward to smash into the pirate at his back.

Elizabeth shut her eyes once again, smiling now. *Leonhardt will win.*

"Isolde." After personally teaching the pirates that they had a total of fifty-four finger bones on both hands combined and driving them down the hill, Leonhardt approached Elizabeth, wiping sweat from his brow.

Elizabeth was closing his eyes waiting for him, just as he had instructed.

"Lizzie." Although it was the summer breeze, the night breeze in the sea was still cold. Leonhardt took off his jacket and put it over Elizabeth's shoulder, calling her name again. "You can open your eyes now."

Their food had all gone cold now. Leonhardt let out a deep sigh and sat on his knees in front of her.

"...Leon..." Elizabeth opened her eyes. At the same time, the tears that she had been holding under her eyelids started flowing down her cheeks to her chin. "I'm okay." Elizabeth sniffled and as her eyes met Leonhardt's, she nodded fervently.

There was a bloodstain on Leonhardt's cheek. "...Did you get hurt?"

Startled by Elizabeth's question, Leonhardt took out a handkerchief and rubbed his cheek. "I don't think it's my blood."

"...I'm upset."

"I'm sorry for making you worry."

Elizabeth shook her head as she sincerely made an angry face. "I... I also wanted to do something. I wanted to protect Leon, too. At least, I didn't want to be a burden..."

If the pirates hadn't kept their promise, she would've become their hostage and held Leon back. She felt helpless. A surge of anger and grief rushed through her. Both during the champagne tower incident at the welcoming reception and now, Leonhardt prioritized Elizabeth over his own body. If this went on, she might end up being a burden to him for the rest of their lives. A useless existence, holding back someone as amazing as Leonhardt. Elizabeth started to hate herself so much a wave of nausea crept up her throat.

"I'm okay," Leonhardt once again told Elizabeth in a gentle manner.

Elizabeth opened her mouth to refute, but Leonhardt moved faster to place a gentle kiss on her forehead, repeating the oath he pledged thousands of times whenever he swung his sword. "As long as I can protect you, I am going to do anything."

A large firework shot up behind Leonhardt, daring to covet the stars beside it as it threw itself into the sky, bursting in its throes of despair. It knew that no matter how much it tried, it could never grab the shadow of the star, let alone pierce the skies. As the firework blew its whole body into shards and sparks and fell into the sea, Leonhardt smiled.

Elizabeth roughly rubbed her tearful eyes with her sleeves to try to engrave that sight in her eyes. When she closed her eyes, she felt like Leonhardt would disappear in the darkness along with the fireworks, so she didn't even want to blink.

"The fireworks... have... started..." She wanted to say more, but her mouth wouldn't move. She wanted to thank him or tell him she was scared. Pathetic. She lowered her head.

A small and round mark dashed on her skirt, a shadow of the fireworks. Leonhardt sat by Elizabeth's side and took her hand. His hand was a bit damp from sweat, but it was very warm and reassuring.

Elizabeth stared up at Leonhardt as he watched the fireworks. Her heart, which had just started to calm, began to pound again. Was he feeling the same?

Beside her, Leonhardt was holding back the urge to steal a glance at Elizabeth. He didn't care much about the fireworks. He just wanted to look at her and check for himself that she was safe, so there was no way he could pay any attention to the rainbows lighting up the sky over the sea. Fortunately, Elizabeth seemed absorbed in the fireworks. She was smiling brighter than the stars, as calm as the shadow of the moon reflected on the waves. Rather than feeling relieved, Leonhardt felt concerned and anxious. How could he keep her smile that way even inside the imperial court?

"So pretty..."

You're prettier, Leonhardt wanted to say, but instead tightened his grip on Elizabeth's hand. His heart was pounding in a different way from when he was swinging his sword, fighting between life and death. Was she feeling the same way? Leonhardt let Elizabeth's head lean on his shoulder.

In the end, Leonhardt and Elizabeth were scolded for over three hours. They were also banned from going out. The only places they could go to were inside the mansion and within the imperial family's private beach. Until the day their vacation ended, they were strictly not allowed to go to any other place.

"Then what about the theater for the play?"

"We'll allow that since you will be with us adults then. But other than that, absolutely not!"

In front of his sincerely furious father, Leonhardt could only nod his head in silence. Elizabeth was also being reprimanded by the empress that they had acted carelessly.

"...Still, I acknowledge the fact that you managed to protect the lady with your own strength. Along with the presence of the pirates."

Leonhardt's head hung low as he listened to the emperor, but he lifted his it a little upon hearing this. But the emperor's fury didn't look like it would subside anytime soon.

"You must be tired, so have a rest. Don't act carelessly anymore. Leonhardt, you are my one and only son before you are this nation's one and only heir. There is no parent who wouldn't worry when their son disappears."

"...I apologize, father."

Seeing Leonhardt's sincerely apologetic expression, the emperor shook his head, looking exhausted. He gestured for his son to go.

As they left the empress' room, Leonhardt and Elizabeth exchanged glances and sighed in unison. "It was our fault this time. Right?"

"Yes..."

"To think they would forbid us from going out. Still, I'm glad we can still at least go to the beach," Leonhardt said with a hint of resignation.

"As long as we're with some adults...?"

"That's true, but I really wanted to show you the fireworks yesterday."

Elizabeth lifted her head and stared at Leonhardt. "Thank you," she murmured, fiddling on the clamshell necklace she wore.

Leonhardt perked an eyebrow. "I couldn't hear you. What did you say?"

Elizabeth lifted her head suddenly scowling, "Crown Prince Leonhardt is a dummy!"

She scurried out to her room, leaving him alone. *Such treasonous words!* Yet, Leonhardt smiled broadly.

After returning to her own room, Elizabeth fell onto her bed and sniffled. Her emotions lately had been like an unpredictable wind, ready to snuff out any small flame of joy. A sense of uneasiness fell over her, making her body feel heavy.

Playing with the seagulls with Her Majesty the Empress, holding hands with Leonhardt while looking around the night market, buying the clamshell necklace which was said to be a charm for lovers... She had fun the entire day, so why was she feeling like this all of a sudden?

She was running her mouth and saying hurtful words again. She felt like everything was her fault, her feelings out of control, and the whole situation left her heart hurting. If she couldn't even control her own feelings, what was she supposed to do?

Elizabeth clenched her hands into fists and repeatedly punched an innocent pillow. Her forehead burned where Leonhardt had kissed it. Her hand that he had held seemed to now hold a flame. Remembering the time Leonhardt told her that he was fine, silhouetted by the fireworks that poured down like rain, made a corner of her heart throb. Elizabeth was the only one who didn't know that in her little heart, a seed had taken root and bloomed into a magnificent flower called love.

THE WHITE BOUQUET & FROM THE SEA

CHAPTER FORTY

Although they felt bitter that the emperor told them to only play within the approved bounds, they acknowledged their carelessness and reflected on their errors. But that effort vanished overnight like seaweed swept away by a tidal wave. In its place was their excitement about the sea and their anticipation for everything new. Even though the emperor was a bit dumbfounded by their excitement, he couldn't interrupt such joy. He could only shake his head and rub the back of his neck, trying not to worry.

Hearing that the Crown Prince and his fiancée had come to visit, the navy sent a small present. Two sets of clothes inside a white box with sharp edges on each corner. One of the outfits was for their future master, Leonhardt, and the other was for Elizabeth. As Leonhardt looked at the coat with fancy epaulets and imitation badges, he gave a bitter smile. Judging by the number of stars on the epaulet, it was a coat for an admiral. The servants helped Leonhardt dress up for the occasion. He admired the clothing in the mirror. A small swell of pride filled his chest as he thought that not slacking off on sword training had been worthwhile. When he tucked his chin and lifted his head, wearing a suddenly serious expression befitting a soldier, the young admiral in the mirror made the same expression.

On the other hand, Elizabeth was wearing a dress that would surely start a new trend in high society. The white gown, made of a slightly heavy fabric for a summer dress, had its skirt pleated with deep blue lines spaced meticulously. Seeing the elaborately calculated and ironed skirt pleats as well as the golden buttons on the chest, reminded Elizabeth of a navy uniform. The six golden buttons were also placed precisely, with orderly gaps between each.

Of all the items accompanying the dress from the box, she most liked the scarf meant to decorate her collar. On her dress was the navy's signature square-shaped sailor collar. The two lines along the edge of the collar were gracefully curled like a boat that had changed direction.

"Would you like to wear a ribbon or a tie, my lady?"

Elizabeth chose the tie without hesitation. At the ends of the scarf—tied around her neck just like any other sailor's—were some small pearl decorations. With a pair of lace socks and black Mary Janes, as well as a small sailor hat placed askew on her head, Elizabeth was all ready to go out.

"Leon!"

"Lizzie!"

Both of them widened their eyes, speechless when they saw each other. Elizabeth looked just like a fairy of the white waves that had climbed onto a ship for a brief moment. Elizabeth's long silver hair was tied into two donut-shaped buns atop her head. The small sailor hat between them was like a crown. She had to wear a petticoat because of the weight of her skirt. But thanks to it, her skirt was puffed up like the sail of a boat blown in the wind. The blue scarf, matching her blue eyes, was tied in the same way navy sailors wore theirs. She looked determined and energetic, and Leonhardt felt relieved.

At the same time, seeing Leonhardt wear the sailors' signature triangular hat and a uniform made Elizabeth's cheeks blush. His violet eyes that were settled low and dignified, but also contained kindness and gentleness that only Elizabeth could see, gazed affectionately at her. Leonhardt had grown up so much that it would no longer be suitable to call him a boy. So, seeing his face from this close felt so new to Elizabeth. Leonhardt was growing up to be a fine young man who suited the word "beautiful," with the thin and elegant lines shaping his nose and jaw and cheekbones—previously hidden by baby fat. The natural dignity that came from being raised as a crown prince, the gaze of a ruler, the hidden power—it all fit neatly with the strong image from the formal uniform. He reminded her of a fairytale ocean prince.

Leonhardt held out his hand, but Elizabeth reacted a beat later. "Lizzie?"

Elizabeth just stared at Leonhardt in a daze. She then snapped out of it and grabbed his hand and hurried down the stairs. She felt like if she didn't run ahead of him, he would find out how red her face was.

"You two look good."

"Lady Elizabeth, it suits you very much."

The adults, who had been waiting for the young pair, exclaimed joyfully at the sight of them. They clapped lightly in approval. The navy sailors displayed their courtesy according to the naval style towards Leonhardt, who was to be their master in the future. Leonhardt was taken aback for a moment, but after exchanging glances with the emperor, he nodded and accepted their greetings in the naval style as well.

Today was the day of the small party with the navy crew.

"We're going to hold an onboard party this last day. Isn't that exciting?"

"Onboard party?"

The empress, in her elegant blue dress, nodded thoughtfully. "It's a party held aboard a ship. The sound of waves will replace the orchestra, and the setting sun and stars will shine more beautifully than any chandelier!"

Elizabeth beamed, mimicking the empress' excitement.

It was no exaggeration to say that almost all seafood was presented at the party venue, including clams, prawns, and lobsters baked in plenty of butter.

"It's all seafood, but I don't see any living ones."

"Yes, Your Highness. Her Majesty the Empress has not been eating raw food in the imperial palace as well, so we made plans and prepared food that is hotter than the summer sun for today."

"She hasn't been eating raw seafood?"

"It is probably because of the heat. Nonetheless, we are planning to prepare Your Highness' favorite oyster for the onboard party."

Leonhardt made small talk with the cook, who was watching the party venue from the corner, looking proud.

As someone who grew up by the sea, the empress especially loved seafood dishes. Among them, her favorite was fresh sliced abalone and fresh small octopus dipped into olive oil and salt. Those dishes were considered strange even in her hometown. Obviously, the late empress didn't approve of such dishes that didn't suit the dignity of the imperial court. However, this was her hometown. Even if they were considered strange, she could eat them as much as she wanted.

But she's been refusing to eat her favorite food? Leonhardt had a bad feeling. He went to Elizabeth, who was already fitting in with the navy sailors.

"Oh! Here you are. Your Highness, we were just listening to the lady's story."

"Story?"

"We heard about how you faced the pirates to protect the lady at the festival yesterday. Wow... His Highness has become a real man now!"

"Th-that's...!"

"Pirates?" The emperor, tilting his wine glass with the admirals, turned his gaze over when he heard the word. The navy sailors, who were already tipsy with rum, wine, or both at once, started to ramble about the Crown Prince's heroic victory against the pirates, forgetting who was in front of them.

"...So, Admiral, the pirates have been operating on land as well these days?"

"Ugh... We have no excuse. We shall wipe them all out before His Highness goes back to the imperial palace."

"I am not blaming you. This is a joyous occasion, so we should put off the heavy talk until tomorrow. I'll be hearing the rest of the story of how the amazing Crown Prince saved Lady Elizabeth."

As the admiral planned to tie those flippant navy sailors on top of the sail later, he moved along with the emperor.

"Okay, okay. Let's not be like this and give us a show! Your Highness!"

"Raaawr! I'm a horrible pirate! If His Highness doesn't come at me seriously, I shall do something rude and imprudent to Lady Elizabeth!"

"What are you guys trying to do?!" Leonhardt's face grew pale.

The adults around them just watched, waiting nearby to step in if needed be. Elizabeth, who was somehow giggling in the middle of the navy sailors, tilted her head as she wondered what the real gentlemen of the sea—reeking of alcohol—were going to do.

"We are going to talk about what happened to the lady and His Highness on the night of the fireworks festival to the whole ocean. To the point that Manannán, the God of the Sea, could hear us!"

"You guys!" Leonhardt's face turned deep red in an instant.

The sailors let out a boisterous laugh as they exchanged glances with each other and surrounded Leonhardt with silverware in hand. It was an action that could be interpreted as a threat against the imperial family, but everyone was so drunk that they just let it off with a laugh, thinking that they couldn't do anything with a spoon.

"You impertinent brutes...! You guys! Wake up and realize what you're trying to do! Are your heads made of a seagull's nest?!" The admiral, who was beginning to sober up, told the navy sailors off with a smack to their heads. He pressed their shoulders down to force them to bow in front of the emperor and the Crown Prince and started to beg for forgiveness on all fours.

The emperor tried to hide his laughter with a serious expression. He handed down judgment with as serious a tone as he could manage towards the people who had aimed their weapons at the Crown Prince. "It is disgraceful to look down on the Crown Prince. It is even more of an insult towards the imperial family to face him with a mere spoon. I give you permission. Take out your swords!"

"Long live His Majesty the Emperor!"

"Father!"

"Your Majesty!" The drunken navy sailors all cheered without exception as they took out their swords.

Even if they were just ceremonial swords, it wouldn't end with just bruises if an adult was determined to stab him. Leonhardt glared at the emperor resentfully. He noticed the empress leaning on the emperor playfully. Everyone around him was enjoying this moment. Leonhardt took a deep, slow breath. *Fine... As long as I can make Elizabeth smile... I just have to sacrifice my body and become an actor...*

Leonhardt took out a decorative sword and got in position. The navy sailors exclaimed excitedly and commented on the Crown Prince's fighting stance. They began to offer tips on how he should stand.

Elizabeth had taken a seat on top of a huge rum barrel. She watched the scene with a smile. She called, "Leon, hang in there! You must win!"

"Your Highness! Even your fiancée has cheered for you. You can't lose!"

"We have no intention to cut some slack for you though!"

Leonhardt gave a bitter smile and leaped forward. The drunk navy sailor with a smooth tongue started to recount his action in an elegant manner as if it were a song by a minstrel. It was a party that was only possible because it was held in the empress' hometown instead of the imperial palace.

"Ugh! Your Highness, your sword is quite sharp!"

"But your back is open!"

"You guys...!" Leonhardt was conflicted. Was it okay to take out his aura when there were so many people around? Elizabeth wanted him to win. Also, no matter how impressive a story it was, he didn't want another man to carelessly sing out her name.

Just a little... as long as they don't find out... just a... Leonhardt thought as he drew his aura out a little. However, there was one thing that he had overlooked.

"Your Highness? That's... Don't tell me..."

"It's... a-aura... How come... His Highness could..."

"This is! So like! So... So like..."

"Crown Prince. Explain."

Leonhardt was perplexed at the fact that the aura he wanted to draw out just a little was now covering the decorative sword like it was burning. Seeing the aura, which showed its presence so strongly that he couldn't say they were seeing it wrong, sobered up the drunk sailors.

"When I was trying to... protect Elizabeth..." Leonhardt mumbled.

CHAPTER
FORTY-ONE

With the empress' homecoming party doubling as a party to celebrate the Crown Prince's awakening as a sword master, the atmosphere became even more excited. The navy sailors' eyes all lit up at the long-awaited opportunity to spar with a sword master, and Leonhardt kept swinging his sword without mercy for Elizabeth's honor. The emperor chuckled proudly at his son, who won the battle against more than half of the troops attending the party. The admiral and other officials offered congratulatory drinks to the emperor, saying that the future of the empire was bright.

The highlight of the party was the completely drunk sailors performing an elaborate tap dance. The sailors first started to practice tap dance to cope with the more boring parts of voyages and to keep up their flexibility and strength, but now it had become something they were quite proud of and unashamed to perform for formal occasions.

Elizabeth expressed her admiration and clapped her hands as she watched them dance—so quickly and precisely it looked like all their legs were one. She had never seen such a dance before in the imperial palace, so the sailors started to talk her into letting them teach her the steps right in front of Leonhardt.

Leonhardt glared at the hand the sailor held out to Elizabeth.

"Oh dear! Seems like this is not possible due to how scary His Highness' gaze is?"

The sailors laughed boisterously again and drank.

"How can navy sailors capture the specters of the sea when they look like that? Lizzie, come over here. You'll get drunk too if you stay over there."

Seeing Leonhardt agitated by the sailors' words made Elizabeth giggle. She went over to his side. "This is my first time at this kind of party."

"Are you having fun?"

"Very much!"

"That's a relief. Shall we go and express our gratitude to mother?" Leonhardt grabbed Elizabeth's hand and began to look around the party for the empress. They found her, tipsy, standing at the emperor's side with her usual calm expression.

"Mother!"

"Mm... Hmm? Oh, it's my babies. Are you done playing?"

"Mother, you don't look so good. Are you not feeling well..."

The empress took a moment to reply, "It's been a long time since I've been to such a joyous party, so I'm just a little intoxicated by the atmosphere. Don't worry too much, my babies."

"Mother…"

"My love, what's the matter?" The emperor, who had been taking in all the congratulatory drinks given to him, finally noticed that the empress' complexion was not normal. He called for people to help find a place for the empress to rest. "This is such a good day, but your expression does not look so good, my love."

"Is that… so? Actually, I… do feel a little unwell…"

"Hmm… it might be because you were surprised to see Leon, that boy, take out his sword just now. You're a sensitive soul, my love. Empress, why don't you go back first to take a rest?"

She placed her hand on her forehead, her complexion looking pale. Slowly, she nodded, saying, "I think I will have to do that. Your Majesty, please do not drink too much."

"You there, take the empress back to rest. My love. I will join you soon. Take care." The emperor kissed the back of the empress' hand before letting the servant lead her away.

Leonhardt watched as the empress took unsteady steps away. Uneasiness made his stomach twist. *Has the future not changed after all? Even if the tragedy can be prevented, is mother destined to not live passed this summer?* As Leonhardt watched the empress' back get farther and farther, his heart sank, and he stretched his hand the way she had gone.

"Leon...?" Elizabeth was by his side.

"It's nothing. I'm just worried since this is mother's long-awaited party, yet she feels under the weather..."

"I will call for a doctor if necessary, so no need to worry, Crown Prince."

"I also hope that you don't get too drunk as mother said, father. I can even bet that when we go back to the Palace, the rumor that I became a sword master would arrive before us."

The emperor grinned and tried to ruffle Leonhardt's hair, but he realized that he had grown too big for him to do that. He just let his hand hover awkwardly. "You've grown well."

"Pardon?"

"Nothing. Just go and take care of your fiancée. If those rascals joke around too far, it'll be troubling for everyone."

"L-Lizzie!" Leonhardt took a glance where the emperor was pointing. He rushed over to where Lizzie was about to drink from a glass in the shape of a small alcohol barrel.

"This is just water. Why were you so surprised that you ran over?"

"It's a relief it's just water. What would you do if it were alcohol? You're just going to drink it?"

"I have a nose. Do you think I can't differentiate between alcohol and water?"

Leonhardt took a deep sigh before giving a glare at the navy sailors who dared to give the Crown Prince's fiancée some water that looked like alcohol.

Thinking that Leonhardt was overreacting, Elizabeth pouted. "Anyway, I learned tap dance from those people. Do you want to see?"

"You learned it in that short of a time?"

"Do you want to see or not?"

Defeated, Leonhardt frowned but joined the sailors to watch Elizabeth. She bounced skillfully on her toes, tap-tapping so quickly. Elizabeth moved incredibly proficiently for someone who had just learned the dance of the sea for the first time.

"How was it?" she asked, out of breath.

Leonhardt clapped his hands with all his heart, so hard his palms started stinging.

Hours went by, and on and on, everyone raised their glasses for the emperor, the empress, the Crown Prince, and his fiancée.

"Empress, are you still not feeling well?" The emperor gently pressed the back of his hand against the empress' cheek.

The empress shook her head.

"Shall I call for a doctor?"

"I am fine. Why is Your Majesty back already when it's an occasion that doesn't come often?"

"How can I drink alcohol when my love is lying down like this?" The emperor held the empress' hand, his brow furrowed.

"It's just... I guess I got too excited by coming home. I'm not even a child anymore."

"Speaking of children, that boy Leonhardt, he's grown so big that it feels off to pat his head. Did you know that, my love?"

"Of course. I've also heard reports that recently, he has been plagued with worry as Elizabeth enters adolescence."

"Oh dear. I hope the lady will at least not cut down a perfectly fine tree."

"Would Elizabeth really do that?" The empress chuckled.

"The children have already... grown so big that it's awkward to call them children."

After the empress sat up with the emperor's help, she smiled and closed her eyes to feel a reliable and warm embrace from her back. "Do you remember? The day we first met, and the moment we met the second time."

"I remember everything. The only thing in my memory is just my love after all."

"Are those children feeling happy at this moment?"

The emperor linked his hand with the empress and patted the back of her hand to reassure her. "I guarantee that those kids will remember this summer for the rest of their lives."

"That... would be great..."

As the emperor saw the empress' eyes flickering close, he laid her down again. Recently, there had been reports that the empress had been unusually drowsy. She started feeling unwell in front of the seafood that she liked so much, and she would spend half of the day pale and sleeping. The emperor was extremely worried about whether something had happened to his beloved empress.

Not too far away, Leonhardt's heart was heavy with anxiety. "Lizzie... Lizzie...?"

The navy sailors finally messed up. The image of the sailors gathered with their heads on the ground with one word from the admiral was quite the spectacle, but Leonhardt didn't have time to appreciate it.

"Leon... It's Leon... Hehe."

"Uh-huh... yes, I am Leon, so... why don't we go back to our rooms and rest?"

"I'm... having so much fun... It's so fun... so fun... but..."

Fearing that she would make a slip of the tongue, Leonhardt picked up her drooping body. He scolded, "Admiral, I'll leave you to take action against the men who dared to make the Crown Prince's fiancée drink water spiked with alcohol."

"By all means, Your Highness. Under the name of Manannán, the God of the Sea, I will make this a summer they will never forget for the rest of their lives."

"I trust you." Leonhardt carried Elizabeth on his back and headed to her room.

Elizabeth, who was breathing softly in his ears, was so light that it felt like she would turn into foam if he didn't hold her tight. After laying her down on her bed, Leonhardt was going to let the maids take over for the rest and leave.

"Leon... don't go..."

"Lizzie..." He thought she had been asleep. Elizabeth's eyes were slightly open as she gripped onto Leonhardt's sleeve.

"Do you want a glass of water?"

"One that's not spiked with alcohol."

"How did that happen?"

"I don't know either… It was just… transparent, and had no odor, so I just drank it…"

"Do you know how surprised I was when I heard? I thought you were once again…"

"Once again?" She drank the cool water and blinked at him.

I thought you were once again poisoned and collapsed. I'm so scared of you dying in my stead. Leonhardt bit his lip. He managed, "Once again… getting in trouble…"

Elizabeth, looking sullen, passed the empty cup to the maid and murmured, "Sorry" to Leonhardt.

"Huh?"

"I said I'm sorry for making you worry."

"Just don't do it again. It's fine."

"Leon is always like that."

"Like what?"

Elizabeth answered only after she returned from being helped by the maid to change out of her party dress and wear a light shawl over her saliva. "You always accept, approve, and tell me it's fine no matter what I do."

"That's because I want Lizzie to have fun and be happy…"

"Then what about Leon?"

"Me?"

Elizabeth grabbed Leonhardt by the collar and pulled him.

Just what alcohol was spiked in the water that Elizabeth's lips still exhaled its scent?

"Since it seems like Leon will be happy if I die, will you give me permission if I say I want to die?"

"L-Lizzie, first, let me go... Why are you suddenly saying that?" Even if Leonhardt was choked up, he didn't readily touch Elizabeth's hand.

Before he knew it, Elizabeth was tearing up again. She started to pour out all the things she had been holding in her heart. "I had so much fun, but what about Leon? Did Leon have fun? Were you happy? What does Leon really like to do? Making me have fun? Is Leon a clown? I... I wish Leon would enjoy doing something else instead of making me have fun. At this rate, I feel like I'm a rare and precious jewel or something. The kind of jewel that gets laid down on a velvet cushion, dusted off with a feather duster and polished with silk every day!"

"Lizzie...?" Leonhardt listened to her but tried to think of it as something temporary, a burst of emotion from puberty.

"I also... I also want to make Leon have fun... but I don't know how to... because Leon always does everything first..."

I'm already having fun and happy enough just by seeing you safe in front of me and pouring out your heart honestly like this. Leonhardt handed Elizabeth a handkerchief in cold sweat. "Can I say something, Lizzie?"

Elizabeth nodded with her face buried in the handkerchief.

"Every day, I would go back and forth between heaven and hell, dozens and thousands of times just because of your gaze, your breath, and your movement. That is how precious you are to me. Is it so bad that I want to make such a precious person have a little more fun, make her smile happily, and help her do whatever she wants?"

Elizabeth shook her head instead of answering.

"My precious Lizzie. I can do anything for you as long as you allow me to. So, if you want to make me have fun... Just... just give me a smile. That's all I need." Leonhardt bent down on one knee.

"Leon... is so bad," Elizabeth muttered after a while as she removed her face from the handkerchief.

"Drink another glass of water, then have a rest. Let's make a sandcastle tomorrow at the beach."

"I told you I'm not a child..." Elizabeth complained as Leonhardt tugged the blanket over her.

"Good night, my precious Lizzie." Leonhardt kissed Elizabeth's forehead good night and backed out of the room.

Elizabeth sat back up and put her hand on her forehead, where Leonhardt had kissed her on just now.

"...Leonhardt is really a dummy."

CHAPTER
FORTY-TWO

The empress seemed fully recovered just the following day. Strolling along the path to the beach, she held Elizabeth's hand and smiled... as if what had been worrying Leonhardt and the emperor so much had been a lie. A few servants followed behind her carrying some drawing tools.

"The sea is a grand being who gives much and takes much," the empress said.

Upon hearing these words, Elizabeth raised her head to look at the horizon. The sand beneath her was swept away each time the water surged forward, and the waves passed over her feet before receding, eliciting a strange feeling within her.

The empress was drawing Elizabeth, who was preoccupied with watching the blue sea ripple into white with each wave, breaking into long, clear fingers that brushed against the fine sand. Her large sketchbook was filled with images of Elizabeth and Leonhardt drawn with charcoal. The two were building a sandcastle as she observed, but they became disappointed when a bigger wave swept through. It crashed over the structure so that the little towers collapsed and crumbled. They began to watch the seawater and seaweed accumulating between the black rocks instead.

And then, at the time when the sun was glaring down at them, they came to the water's edge to soak their feet and kick their toes in the cool blue waves. The empress recorded all of those in her sketchbook.

"Do you really not remember what happened last night?"

"I don't remember. All I know is I drank something the sailor uncle gave me..."

"That's fine if you don't. That's okay."

"Is it really okay?"

Leonhardt awkwardly nodded.

Without Leonhardt knowing, Elizabeth secretly wrote both his and her names on the sand. It had been only one night, yet she felt she would never forget the time they embodied Tristan and Isolde.

"Lizzie?" Leonhardt turned around when he noticed that the spot beside him was empty.

Elizabeth knelt nearby, scribbling something on the sand. He tried to approach her, curious about what she was doing, but then a wave sneaked up on them, sweeping her sketches away from him.

"Leon, what's that tower-like thing over there?" Elizabeth was still sitting on the sand, but she gestured at something in the distance.

"The lighthouse? At night, that tower gets lit up bright enough so that a ship could see even from far away and sends signals."

"Signals?"

"Yesterday... Oh right, now that I think about it, with the fireworks and everything else, we've never had the chance to see the sea at night. Look, you can see the horizon clearly now, right?" Leonhardt said, sitting by Elizabeth's side along the line.

"It's really pretty the way the parts where the sky and the ocean collide would sparkle."

"I told you... your eyes are exactly that color."

Elizabeth jabbed Leonhardt's side, urging him to proceed with the explanation.

"When it's night, the sea becomes a mirror of the sky. Obviously, it feels fantastic to cleave through the stars of the night sky, but... the problem lies in the rocks and mountains being hidden in the dark even though they could be seen clearly in the day."

"And that's why the lighthouse sends signals? Like 'this place is dangerous,' or 'the harbor is over here'?"

"I like that Lizzie is so smart."

With a sudden splash, water smacked Leonhardt's face. The wave that slapped his face in Elizabeth's place was cold and haughty as it retreated back into the sea.

"Then is Leon my lighthouse?"

"Huh?"

Elizabeth followed Leonhardt and sat on a spot that the waves wouldn't reach. As she watched the waves tickling her toes, bringing the fine sand along like they were spoils of war, Elizabeth leaned her face on her knees. "When I was at the duke's residence... I feel like I only lived with the purpose of being the perfect lady befitting Leon no matter what."

"Why are you thinking about that...?" Leonhardt asked gently.

Elizabeth spoke calmly, "I just learned manners and wore stuffy clothes, just like mother ordered me to. I thought that as long as I did that, it would all be over once I became the Crown Princess and then the empress."

Leonhardt listened intently, maintaining his silence to give her the space she needed.

"But one day, Leon showed me a path. You taught me. Until then, I couldn't tell what was right or wrong by myself, how to think for myself and that I have the power to choose. Do you remember?"

"The day we charged into the duke's residence in the morning?"

Elizabeth nodded, saying, "I was so scared because it felt like my world was crumbling down. I wanted to ask someone whether this was the right thing, but there was no one who would answer."

"But weren't you the one who laid down the order to open the door?"

"I could do that because Leon was the one who taught me how. I think I vaguely realized that I was a human, not a doll who could only move as told, the moment the butler asked for my permission." Elizabeth wriggled her toes. Both of her little toes were slightly bent towards her soles, all because of the shoes that she wore when she was way too young. Leonhardt had repeatedly thanked the gods that the doctor had diagnosed that it wouldn't really affect the long-term condition of her feet or her ability to comfortably walk.

"Leon was the one who told me where to go. That's why Leon is my lighthouse," Elizabeth said brightly, smiling as she looked at Leonhardt.

With that one smile, a spray of sunlight hit the swaying waves and broke into a hundred, a thousand blinding lights.

"Thank you, Leon." Elizabeth said before she stood up and ran to the empress. She couldn't tell whether it was stinging because the white sand was sticking onto her wet soles, or because a corner of her heart was aching.

"Oh my, what's wrong, sweetheart?" The empress welcomed her and gave her a seat and a cool drink. The glass was created using one of this place's specialties of glasswork techniques in the shape of a fishbowl. Instead of pebbles, it was filled with round-shaped fruits boiled in sugar in a blueberry juice sipped through a straw with a fish decoration.

Having talked for so long under the sun left Elizabeth parched, compelling her to quickly empty her glass. The ice cubes clattered in the empty glass. The ice, enchanted to prevent melting, bore a spell scarcely visible to anyone but the wealthiest of nobles.

"Are you drawing?"

The empress nodded. "Do you want to see?"

Elizabeth flinched before nodding her head. Her eyes had been full of curiosity as she looked at the drawing of Leonhardt and herself drawn with rough lines on the sketchbook. "Wow... it looks so real, not like a drawing."

The empress' sketchbook was full of the imperial court from her perspective. On the very first page was a young Leonhardt Elizabeth had never seen before. "Is this His Highness the Crown Prince?"

"This is when Leon was five years old. Don't you think he still has the same eyes?" With a tender laugh, the empress talked about how Leonhardt behaved just like a small tyrant and was prone to making trouble in the imperial court up to the night before he met Elizabeth.

"Somehow, he seems like... a different person from the Leon today."

He was the same Leonhardt who sat while resting his chin on the window, but he was somehow different. For some time, Elizabeth looked between the pages to figure out what was so different.

"This is Leon before meeting you, my Dear, and this is Leon the day after he met you."

"What? How can his attitude change so much in one day... Ahem, ahem. Pardon me. Please forgive my slip of tongue."

"It's not a slip of tongue if it's the truth. But keep it a secret from Leon, okay?" The empress pressed her head against Elizabeth's as she whispered with a mischievous smile.

Elizabeth giggled with her and nodded.

"This is..."

"Ahem, ahem! Why don't we look at the next page?"

It was a picture of His Majesty the Emperor sleeping soundly on a long sofa with nothing but a thin blanket. The empress' face flushed as she flipped through the sketchbook pages, then flipped again, then flipped again.

"Your Majesty sure drew a lot of His Majesty."

"Can you keep this between us?"

Elizabeth looked off at the sea far away as she nodded. She couldn't be sure since the pages were flipped too quickly, but the emperor in the drawings always smiled at the empress.

Only after flipping through numerous pages did Leonhardt and Elizabeth finally appear again. It was the day of the welcoming reception, when Leonhardt had presented Elizabeth with a flower that would never wilt and asked for her permission to be able to make her happy. When Elizabeth realized what expression she had at that time, her cheeks turned red, and she started fanning her face with her hand.

"On this day, Leonhardt and Elizabeth fell in love."

"Pardon? We did?"

The empress nodded, then quickly noticed something peculiar. The two conjoined trees, which had only started to grow verdant leaves by turning their thick stems towards the sky, seemed as if they were not fully aware of each other's feelings yet.

"What is love?" Elizabeth asked, unsure.

The empress flipped to a new page and gave Elizabeth a charcoal.

"Y-Your Majesty?"

"It's okay, you can just draw whatever is in your heart, dear."

"But I've never done this before..."

"It was also difficult for me to even draw a line at first. It's enough as long as you yourself can recognize it."

Hesitantly, Elizabeth pressed the charcoal against the white paper. Unlike with a pen, the feeling and sound of brushing the charcoal against the paper was a little rough and aggressive. However, what was left behind by the charcoal was a line as soft as a cloud. Elizabeth quickly became invested in drawing with the charcoal that she sat a little closer to the easel.

Still, she said, "I'm... not sure what to draw."

The empress, who watched her proudly, grinned as she saw Elizabeth's flushed features. She told her, "Something in your heart, something precious, this moment. Anything is fine."

"Something precious..." Elizabeth echoed the empress' words before turning her body around again. She could still remember the person in her heart, the person precious to her, and the times spent with that person even when she closed her eyes. Elizabeth was so absorbed in drawing that she didn't notice her white sleeves had been stained black from the charcoal.

The empress made a small exclamation of awe under her breath as she watched Elizabeth's drawing take shape under her clumsy yet diligent fingers.

"Umm… Your Majesty." After tapping the paper a few times to express the fireworks, Elizabeth once again turned around to look at the empress.

"I want to formally learn how to draw."

"How to draw?" The empress delightfully approved. A noble lady learning how to draw as a hobby was not against etiquette. Even if it were, who could say anything when the empress, who was the head of all ladies in the empire, had given her permission? However, she was curious about the reason. The empress chose to draw because she never wanted to forget the moment when the blue waves of her hometown broke and the wind she felt while riding her horse. Although she couldn't fully reproduce that light and sensation, she was satisfied because she could capture the images of her loved ones instead. Was Elizabeth feeling that way as well?

"Can I ask why you want to start drawing?" she asked her.

Elizabeth couldn't answer easily and was quiet for a while. She only stared at Leonhardt, who had somehow started spearfishing with the servants. The empress smiled, understanding. She asked, "Lizzie, do you like Leon?"

CHAPTER
FORTY-THREE

"I'm... not sure." Elizabeth was at the age to know that what the empress meant by "like" was not a matter of likes and dislikes.

In Elizabeth's world, Leon seemed to be her one and only guiding light. Just like sailors wouldn't point at the North Star and say they like it, maybe Elizabeth also didn't like Leonhardt that way—was what the empress thought.

"Our Elizabeth has grown up so much." The empress stroked Elizabeth's head. "I think it's almost time for me to pass on the crown of the empress."

"That is not true, Your Majesty!" Elizabeth started. "I am still much too lacking to become an empress."

"Lizzie, do you want to be with Leon forever?" The empress' smiled, only half-joking.

Surprised, Elizabeth frowned, suddenly so nervous that her hands shook. "Forever..."

"Each other's pain, happiness, sadness, and joy. Do you think you can share them all together?"

Why is the empress asking these questions? Elizabeth thought, gazing up at the empress' benevolent expression. She hesitated and then asked softly, "Is Your Majesty also sharing all of them with His Majesty the Emperor?"

The empress didn't answer for a while. With an inscrutable smile, she said, "There isn't anyone in the world who wants to share their own sorrow with their loved ones," the empress sighed before continuing. "Sometimes we love each other so much that we would rather hide some things and feel the pain alone."

"Then how did Your Majesty decide to stay with His Majesty forever?"

"Because I like him." The empress' cheeks turned redder than a starfish. "I like and love him enough to endure that suffering, and that is why we are together."

"I... I'm not sure. It sounds like Your Majesty is saying that the feeling of 'liking' means sharing all the emotions together, thus spending the rest of their lives together..."

"And being together despite all those sufferings, is called 'love.'"

"Love?"

The empress nodded.

Elizabeth was growing up. Her body had matured into that of a young woman's, but because she was unfamiliar with the feelings of liking someone and the joys of love, a part of her remained childlike—one that still had a long way to go to reach full adulthood. The empress realized that from now on, there were a great many things she needed to teach the young maiden with naive blue eyes. She said, "Elizabeth. Can you try to close your eyes and think of the Crown Prince?"

Following the empress' instruction, Elizabeth closed her eyes and thought of Leonhardt.

"What do you feel?"

"...It tickles somewhere in my heart. It sways like a sprout being tossed around by a gentle misty rain, and it shakes little by little in a regular interval that feels kind of scary."

"And then?"

"I can't help but keep picturing Leon's smiling face. I keep thinking about the last time... the night we caused great worry to both of Your Majesties... when Leon smiled at me with the fireworks shooting up behind him."

"Elizabeth, will you open your eyes and look into the mirror?"

Following the empress' instruction again, Elizabeth looked into the mirror. The reflection showed her with a bright smile, radiant like a summer sunflower, infectious enough to make anyone else smile.

"If a smile is your first reaction when you think of someone, that is the proof that you like that person."

"Does Your Majesty also always smile when you think of His Majesty the Emperor?"

The empress nodded. "Do you think I only smile? Sometimes I also cry or get angry."

"But you said you smile when you think of someone you like..."

"We reveal all of our other emotions to the person we love."

Elizabeth rubbed her hands together. "I do not understand."

Rather than reproaching the sullen Elizabeth, the empress lightly laughed. "I was the youngest among my siblings. I was born on my Eldest Brother's wedding day, so you could say that it was a bit messy."

When the empress suddenly started talking about her family instead of the "like" feeling, Elizabeth tilted her head.

"I was so adored as the child that was born so late. My family spoiled me, and they would even go across the continent to get the things I wanted. But then, my adolescence came."

"Adolescence?"

"Maybe it was when I was around your age? The youngest of my older brothers just came back from his voyage after years, so we held a banquet. However, by his side was a woman I had never seen before." The empress looked off to the distance, thinking about where her older brother was sleeping, with a sentimental expression. "It was so strange. I understood it in my head, and I should've been happy that my most beloved brother was able to come back safely from across the continent, who had seemingly become the main character of a romantic story that seems like it would only appear in a fairy tale. But then, do you know what I did that day?"

"Wh-what was it that you did...?"

The empress chuckled. It was only a memory now, but at that time, she had been so shocked. "After seeing my older brother embracing that woman first without reserve even though he used to always hug me first whenever he came home, I shut myself inside my room until the day he went on another voyage."

"Huh?" Elizabeth's eyes widened in surprise, finding it hard to believe that Her Majesty the Empress, known for her gentleness and benevolence, would act in such a way!

"My nanny, older brothers, and even my mother and father tried to persuade me, but I still didn't come out of my room. No, I couldn't."

"Wh-why not?"

"My mind understood, but my body wouldn't move. Just like how you are now."

"J-just like me?"

The empress nodded, seeming to understand it all. "Even though I didn't know when I could see him again if I missed this chance. Even though I should've gone to that woman, apologized to her, and told her to take care of my older brother right then and there."

The empress sketched outlines of her brothers with their respective spouses in a corner of her sketchbook as they talked. Regret made the black lines on the paper long and heavy. "Even though I just needed to turn that knob once, even though that was all I needed to do... my body wouldn't move. No matter how desperately my big brother was calling for me from beyond the door, I couldn't open it."

"Your Majesty..."

"Then, on his next voyage, my brother had to be put to sleep for good between the coral reefs with the sound of waves as a lullaby, because I didn't give him my kiss of blessing."

"Your Majesty!"

Elizabeth cried out in a sad voice, almost like death throe. She collected herself with a wavering breath and then explained, "That's why, Elizabeth, be very careful to avoid regrets. You have to think and judge wisely, understanding that not everything you say truly reflects your thoughts, and not every action accurately represents your intentions."

"Did I... do something wrong?" Anxious, Elizabeth tried to read the empress. She couldn't be entirely sure why the empress was telling her all this.

"Far from it... I am merely sharing advice based on my own experiences, hoping to spare you from enduring a difficult adolescence."

"Ado...lescence?"

"An age when you think of spring. The age when you get shy whenever you think of someone's smiling face, and the age when you get upset because nothing is going the way you want and find everything to be displeasing. Doesn't it sound just like the Elizabeth today?"

"Your Majesty, how did you..." A blush creeped up Elizabeth's face. Just like what she said, Elizabeth's heart pounded whenever she thought of Leonhardt's smiling face. There were also countless times when she got upset that nothing was going the way she wanted and regretted it when she made an unplanned, cutting remark.

And that was all because of adolescence?

"It is a natural thing that any human with emotion will go through, so don't worry too much. This empress is in fact rather overjoyed. To think that our young Crown Princess, who used to be just like a doll when she first came to the palace and would just obey whatever the adults told her to do without knowing what she likes or dislikes, could have her heart flutter because of somebody's smile!"

Elizabeth cupped her face with her hands, feeling warmth spread across her cheeks from the empress' words, hotter than the sun's rays.

"Elizabeth, do you like Leonhardt?"

Elizabeth slowly nodded. After listening to the empress, she realized there was no longer anything to ponder. The answer was already there, seemingly already known by everyone around her. After belatedly becoming aware of her feelings, Elizabeth's face reddened even more.

"Then, Elizabeth, do you love Leonhardt?" the empress asked mischievously.

"L-love...?"

"Anyone can 'like' someone, but it's different from 'loving' someone. Can you tell the difference between my love for the sea and my love for His Majesty the Emperor?"

That question was still too complex and subtle for Elizabeth to answer without some thought. The empress just smiled and stroked the girl's head. "Sweetheart, tell me if your feelings change. You still haven't officially become the Crown Princess yet, so you can still see other boys."

"Pardon...?"

"You need to become even a little happier. If Leon isn't qualified or capable of making you happy, isn't it obvious that you need to find someone better?"

"But I…"

"Who could oppose the empress? No, I'll even take responsibility and find someone suitable for you, my dear."

"I… I'm… with Leon… Leon… so…"

"Do you think he's someone who's decent enough to spend the rest of your life with? My son?"

"So… umm… that's…"

I'll really make her cry if I go on. Instead of pushing it even further, the empress pressed the back of her hand against the girl's cheek. "Do you like Leon?"

Elizabeth nodded. She couldn't really understand what it meant to share joy, sorrow, happiness, pain, and other emotions with each other. But she was certain that she wanted to enjoy everything together with him.

"Do you want to be with Leon?"

"I want to… always smile with Leon…"

As if she was satisfied with that answer, the empress smiled as she leaned back. It seemed like her young daughter-in-law had fallen deep in love with her son. She looked forward to seeing Elizabeth figure out what everyone around her already knew, but on the other hand, she also felt a little sorry for Leonhardt. "I see Elizabeth likes Leonhardt a lot."

"Is it... really... like..." Elizabeth stammered. She dipped her head. Even the backs of her ears were red.

The empress nodded. "Yes. Elizabeth likes Leonhardt now. At least, that's what it looks like in this empress' eyes. And Leonhardt also seems to like Elizabeth just as much."

"Leon, too...?" Elizabeth straightened and opened her mouth. To think Leonhardt also liked her! It was something she had never considered before. "Does Your Majesty perhaps also use magic?"

"Huh? Magic?" The empress gave Elizabeth a puzzle. The young woman held her red face in her hands. The empress realized what Elizabeth meant and laughed at how adorable she was.

"Ahaha! Elizabeth, this is not magic."

"Then? Can someone's feelings be seen with the naked eye?" Elizabeth dragged her chair a little closer to the empress, her face was filled with curiosity.

"It's obvious to see when someone likes another person. From their gaze, from the words they say, and from their behavior... they beam as if there was nothing else in this world that could compare."

Elizabeth breathed in sharply. "Does Leon also beam like that when he looks at me?"

The empress nodded, as if it were obvious. Starting from the day he went to the duke's residence for the first time, Elizabeth had always been the focus of Leonhardt's gaze. Even right now, although he might look like he was having fun spearfishing with the knights, he stole glances at Elizabeth and the empress every now and then.

As if her words came true, Elizabeth turned her gaze to the sea just in case and met Leonhardt's eyes at that moment. She averted her gaze and lowered her head in a hurry. "Does His Highness... also know?"

"Know what?" The empress pretended not to understand. From this point on, this was something that Elizabeth had to judge by herself. The child who had a hard time choosing her likes and dislikes as her room was being decorated when she first came to the palace, had now grown big enough to have feelings as complex as an intricate snowflake. The empress just felt so proud of, pleased with, and grateful to Elizabeth.

"That I... umm... might like... His Highness..."

THE WAVES SPLASH, AND THE HEART BEATS

CHAPTER
FORTY-FOUR

"That nobody knows."

"Huh?"

The empress then said with a mischievous laugh, "Why don't you go ask Leon directly?"

"Can I do that?"

I wonder what expression our Crown Prince will make if the person he likes asks him whether he likes her? Even imagining it brought her to a smile. The empress said, "There are times when people can't figure out another person's feelings unless they were told straight, and so many tragedies happen precisely because of such a trivial thing."

"Oh?"

The empress took Elizabeth's shoulders and nodded seriously. "Elizabeth, my sweet daughter-in-law. Take caution so that such tragedies shall not happen."

"I will keep that in mind!"

Leonhardt tilted his head when he saw from afar that the empress was holding Elizabeth's shoulders and making a long speech. He didn't realize that a large wave was rising behind him. It crashed down, drenching him with the cold sea water from head to toe.

"Your Highness! Are you all right?!"

Leonhardt waved his hand to tell them he was fine.

"What are you having so much fun talking about with our daughter-in-law?"

"Your Majesty!"

The emperor, having stepped out briefly earlier, had now returned. The empress excitedly summarized the conversation.

"Hoho, it's already that time for our daughter -in-law? The years really have gone by."

"Haha, what if our Crown Prince gets so surprised he can't sleep tonight?"

"There's no way. I didn't raise my son to be so weak."

"But Your Majesty also froze on the spot for a while when I confessed my feelings. I still remember the moment very clearly, you know?"

"Empress, that time was..."

The empress sipped her juice, smiling with her eyes— the same smile that had made him fall in love with her so many years ago when talks of their marriage were going on.

They only had a few days left to play around all day on the beach. Leonhardt and Elizabeth agreed to focus on making a few more memories they could share with Albert or Mimir when they returned to the palace.

"But aren't we not allowed to go anywhere other than the beach...?"

"That's true, but..." Leonhardt awkwardly scratched the back of his head when Elizabeth came to the point.

"Hey, Leon."

"Hm?"

Elizabeth gulped a little. This moment when they were talking for the last time just before going to bed was the perfect moment for her to put into action what she decided to do during her talk with the empress earlier that day.

"I like you."

"What?"

"Does Leon like me too?"

Leonhardt doubted his ears for a second. What did his beautiful, slender-armed fiancée in her silky white sleepwear just say?

I like you. Those words surged over and over in his ears, just like the crashing waves on the shore at night. Loud and relentless.

What should I say? Leonhardt pondered.

How should I react? Leonhardt was conflicted.

Why was Elizabeth suddenly doing this? The smile on Leonhardt's face disappeared.

Elizabeth watched it all happen, and she was terrified to see that her words caused the smile to vanish from Leonhardt's face. "You don't have to answer!" she stammered. "Sorry, Leon. I said something strange all of a sudden... The empress just... No, it's nothing. Good night!"

Elizabeth didn't even give Leonhardt the chance to answer before she rushed into her room and shut the door. Elizabeth slid down to the floor with her back against the door, burying her face between her knees to calm her pounding heart down. *Did I say something I wasn't supposed to say? Is that why Leon reacted like that?*

The empress had told her that it would definitely be obvious if she looked at his eyes. However, the only emotions she could read from Leonhardt's eyes were perplexity and uneasiness. Even the smile that he always naturally showed her had disappeared. Elizabeth might be clumsy when it came to emotion, but even she knew the good from the bad.

Her fear crept up on her, fueled by the shadows around her and in her mind, consuming every little bit of darkness and growing...

Perhaps, just perhaps. *Could it be that... he doesn't like me?*

A feeling as sharp as an ice pick pierced her heart. A cutting bolt of anxiety so deep it made Elizabeth cover her mouth and shriek.

Was I wrong all along? Am I the only one who likes him? Elizabeth raised her head. Before she knew it, the fear had grown bigger than her body and overshadowed her like a towering length of black seaweed in blue of the sea.

And so, Elizabeth had a nightmare that night.

"I knew this would happen! Even though I've told you so many times that you always, always have to be the best lady!" Her mother was approaching her with a ghastly face, holding a corset in one hand and high heels in the other.

Elizabeth unknowingly took a step backward, then stumbled on something hard and toppled to the floor.

Mother's expression was becoming more and more terrible, her brows sharp, her mouth a hard line. When Elizabeth looked back, she screamed and crawled forward again. She had stumbled on her father's rod. He stalked toward her too, his eyes ablaze.

"Isolde! What is that vulgar movement?!"

"Isolde."

"M-mother... father..."

"I knew this would happen. Show your calf now!" Her mother's lips and eyes looked so strange, oddly sliced to the sides. She dashed at Elizabeth with a whip in hand.

I can't get caught. I have to go! Run!

Her body wouldn't move. Elizabeth screamed and writhed, trying to force her body to *move*.

Pain stabbed through the soles of her feet and the tips of her toes. High heels. The breath was yanked sharply from her lungs, her whole body constricted. The corset suffocated her.

"No!" Elizabeth screamed again and flailed against them.

A cold, white hand snatched at her, then snaked around her ankle and started to pull. Somewhere along the line, the space she was in changed into the all-white room in the duke's residence. A quiet, doll-like lady wearing a showy dress appeared before her, sitting neatly. The lady's eyes were dull, and her chest moved in shallow, tortured breaths. This woman, this stiff ceramic doll, this living corpse—had the same silver hair and blue eyes as Elizabeth.

"Our Isolde, good girl Isolde. Everything is for Isolde's sake. You do understand this mother of yours, right?"

"Yes, mother."

For my sake? Lies! They weren't! They aren't!

"Don't be concerned with that useless girl. I have never given birth to such a crude girl. Our Isolde is a priceless little princess who will be the empress someday!"

"Mother!" Elizabeth cried. It was getting harder and harder to breathe.

"Isolde."

Elizabeth turned around, hiccupping. Her father, his face twisted in anger, lifted the metal rod. "You useless girl! You are a smear our family's honor…!"

Elizabeth closed her eyes and curled up.

"You have to be educated from the start! You need to study!"

"Do as your mother says."

"In the first place, you dare to like His Highness the Crown Prince? Don't be ridiculous! You think such a person would like you?"

"No, no! There's no way! Leon is… Leon is…"

"You don't even know what 'like' is!"

"You couldn't even choose what you like or dislike by yourself!"

"No!" Elizabeth covered her ears, but her parents' sneers endlessly swirled inside her head like a whirlwind. "Leon… Leon… where are you…? Help me…" Elizabeth kept calling his name, an aching desperation overcoming her. She wished so badly that he would appear like magic and take her away from here.

However, such a miracle wasn't happening. Instead, her nightmare only became worse.

"Bye, Elizabeth. I found someone more suited to be the empress than you." Beside Leonhardt stood a woman in a white dress and veil, which he gently lifted.

Beneath it was a bizarre Isolde, her eyes lifeless and her waist no bigger than a fist. A skeletal, broken corpse of a person. She looked at Elizabeth and smirked.

"I have never liked you even once."

"Leon!" Elizabeth scratched the ground with her nails so she could get closer, wailing again, "Please don't go!"

The small shadow soared up from inside the bed curtain. Elizabeth gasped, realizing she was awake. She checked her waist. Fortunately, the only discomfort she felt was her pajamas drenched in cold sweat.

Was it... was it a dream? Elizabeth carefully climbed down her bed. Once her bare feet touched the soft carpet, some sense of relief finally washed through her. She drank a glass of water, trying to cool off her body, which was drenched with sweat. She tried to breathe in the ocean wind through the window, trying her best to forget the nightmare.

Knock, knock, knock.

When she was about to take a seat on the terrace, she heard the knock. Did the screams she let out in her dreams leak into real life? Maybe a maid came out of worry. Elizabeth slowly approached the door.

"Lizzie, Lizzie? Are you okay?"

And she held her breath in front of the doorknob. Outside the door, there was Leonhardt, who had just thrown her away just a moment before.

Leonhardt couldn't sleep. He just tossed and turned and rolled on his bed.

Like. Did she say that knowing what it means? He couldn't even imagine that she would ever say that. The words had been like a sudden attack, knocking out all of his senses in an instant. Judging by how she mentioned his mother, he was sure that the empress was behind some sort of practical joke.

Play tricks on someone else! Leonhardt uselessly kicked his blanket.

To think that when he heard that she liked him, he was first more worried and anxious than happy. Leonhardt lamented his pathetic behavior and tossed his body again, still rolling around on his bed.

Am I... really allowed to hear Lizzie say she likes me? Guilt and regret clutched at him, pulling him down like heavy mud.

What if the like you meant and the like I feel are one and the same? Can I covet you that way? Lizzie, I'm not sure. I helped you smile, I helped you have fun, and I protected you. I resolved to live for your sake, and I've been living that way, but... I'm still not sure. Is it really okay for me to like you? Will I have the right to love you in the future?

Using his arm as a pillow and crossing his legs, Leonhardt let out a deep sigh. When he closed his eyes, Elizabeth's when she said she liked him floated around in his mind. When he opened his eyes, he could see her disappointment in his reaction and her turning, forlorn, back to her room.

After scrambling around in the bed, hugging his blanket, and tossing and rolling... Leonhardt sat up.

Lizzie... Elizabeth was screaming. Leonhardt jumped out of bed and opened the door. Across the hall, Elizabeth's room's door was shut tight. When he pressed his ear against it, he could hear Elizabeth's voice, sounding weak even as she groaned and screamed.

"Lizzie! Lizzie! Open the door, Lizzie!" Leonhardt called, grabbing the door handle. Just how bad a dream was she having to be in so much pain? Leonhardt was determined to wake everyone up just to save her from her dream if push came to shove.

Holding his breath to listen closely to the movements inside the room, Leonhardt winced as Elizabeth suddenly stopped screaming. Feeling anxious, he once again knocked on the door.

Knock, knock, knock!

The solid wooden door announced his visit with a clear, calm sound.

"Lizzie, Lizzie? Are you okay?" When he heard footsteps coming closer, Leonhardt finally breathed again.

But he got no answer in return.

FORTY-FIVE

The pair sat down with their backs against the door between them. Leonhardt could hear Elizabeth's breathing even from behind the solid door, several inches thick, but he couldn't do anything.

Elizabeth didn't know what to do. Should she open the door for him? Or should she pretend nothing happened and just go back to sleep?

Should he open the door by force? Or should he just go back to his room because he already checked that she was fine?

Leonhardt leaned his back even more on the door. "Lizzie... can you hear me?"

Burying her head between her knees and all huddled up, Elizabeth perked her ears.

"You don't... have to answer... so can you just listen to me?" There was no answer this time either, but Leonhardt felt relieved when he noticed that Elizabeth's breathing sounded calm again from beyond the door. He said, "I like you, Lizzie."

Leonhardt looked up at the ceiling, mumbling his confession. "If... the 'like' you mean is not the kind of 'like' that makes you choose blue when you're asked if you prefer red or blue, and if the 'like' you talked about means liking someone romantically... then I also like Lizzie... I like everything about you."

Elizabeth was puzzled. Why then did he make that face earlier when she first told him how she felt?

"Earlier, I didn't say anything because... I was surprised. I was so surprised that I didn't know how to answer..." He lifted his arms. "Oh dang it! Lizzie, think about it. If something you treasure, like a flower you've always liked and taken care of, a sparkling jewel... or even a cherished book, suddenly expressed feelings towards you, how would you react? I'm sure you'd be unbearably surprised, too."

Why are these the best excuses I can think of? Leonhardt let out a long sigh and scratched his nose.

"Am I... something Leon treasures?" It was a soft and faint voice, like a wave sweeping over the fine sand.

Leonhardt smiled bitterly. "I treasure Lizzie so much that I can give you everything even if we were reborn. Aren't you too late in realizing this? That's saddening..."

"Sorry! Then... that means... Leon..."

"I like you. I really like you, Lizzie."

Elizabeth's heart pounded again as she felt she had finally understood the reason why a corner of her heart hurt so much whenever she thought of him. She realized why she would sometimes feel shy whenever her eyes met his, and why he was present in all her happy and precious memories. It was all because she liked Leon.

"Elizabeth."

"Leon..."

"I'm... actually still not sure. Is it okay for me to like you? Just as much as you like me—no. Can I like you even more than that? I'm a greedy person, so I might not even be able to let you go if you let me like you. If you're fine with that... can you allow me to like you?"

Can I like you again? Leonhardt thought as he stared at the pattern on the wallpaper. He had reversed time. He had confidence that he could live only to make her happy. It was the natural thing to do. However, gaining her love was just his greed, wasn't it?

Elizabeth pondered how she should answer him. She didn't understand everything he said, but she at least knew that this was a more complicated problem than picking the color of her curtains. Shouldn't it be okay to like and love someone any way you want simply because you treasure them so much? Because you like them so much that you smile every single time you look at them?

Moreover, Leonhardt was the Crown Prince. The third highest ranking person in the empire. If he wanted, he could've just liked her without needing to ask for her permission. Then why was he asking for it?

"If... I say no, what will Leon do?" Elizabeth suppressed her fear and asked him. From beyond the door, she could hear someone gasping and holding his breath for a second.

"...I'll respect your opinion. If you want to break our engagement..."

"No! I don't want that!"

"Elizabeth."

Without realizing, Elizabeth found herself kneeling, her hands gripping the doorknob.

"I'll... help you a little more. Lizzie, do you want to see me smile? Do you want to stay by my side? Do you want to be with me? Do you think you can accept half of my entire feelings and share half of yours?"

"All of it is fine. I'm fine with everything. I want Leon to smile. I want you to stay by my side like right now. I'm okay with Leon showing any kind of feelings, and I'm also okay with giving all of my feelings. It's okay... it's okay, so..."

"Elizabeth, do you like me?"

Elizabeth pulled the doorknob like she was slipping. Then, with a surprised shout, the face that she longed for so much fell on her lap like a shooting star.

Leonhardt looked up at Elizabeth, his eyes damper and more affectionate than ever. He brushed the back of his hand, which had fingers that had grown thick, against Elizabeth's cheek and wiped away a teardrop.

"I like you... I like you, Leon. I like you the most in the world."

More tears began to fall on Leonhardt's face. Elizabeth sniffled as she covered Leonhardt's eyes with her hands. She wanted to show only her pretty self in front of him.

"It's okay, Lizzie. Don't cry. Obviously, you still look the prettiest in the world to me even when you cry, but... give me a smile. Show your smiling face instead of crying when you're with the person you like. Okay?" Leonhardt carefully took Elizabeth's hand off his face.

His heart, which was already in ashes, began to melt once more seeing her tears. However, Leonhardt suppressed that pain and forced himself to smile, to do the same as he asked of her.

Elizabeth caressed Leonhardt's face and smiled with a lot of effort.

"I like you. I adore you. I pine for you. I'm devoted to you. I yearn for you. What else is there?"

"...All of them mean you like me."

"That is the way I like you. Will you give me permission?"

Elizabeth slowly lowered her head. She got close enough to the point where they could feel each other's breath. Gently, she placed a little kiss on the bridge of his nose. No one told her to do that, and no one taught her to do that, but her body moved by itself. "I'll allow it but promise me something in exchange. That you'll like me for the rest of your life."

"With a pinky promise?"

"Yes."

Leonhardt grinned and raised his hand. Elizabeth then linked her little finger with Leonhardt's to make a promise together.

Leonhardt likes Elizabeth.

Elizabeth likes Leonhardt.

Elizabeth's smile looked like an angel's.

"Umm... Lizzie, am I too heavy?" Leonhardt asked, wondering if it was time for him to get up from her lap.

Elizabeth realized the position they were in. Her face flushed red. "A-are there other people around?"

"No, but..."

Elizabeth decided to pluck up her courage a little more. This was her chance to admire Leonhardt's face since he'd usually be the one looking down at her. "Can we stay like this for a little longer?"

"But you should tell me if I'm too heavy," Leonhardt answered softly. He reached out to Elizabeth's long, soft hair and coiled the tresses around his fingers. If this was a dream, he never wanted to wake up. If this were a nightmare, he hoped that time would stop right here. But her silver hair, glistening like the northern lights, and her smiling blue eyes smiling were too vivid for this to be a nightmare.

"I had a nightmare."

"A nightmare?"

"My parents appeared with their eyes and mouth torn like this, and Leon was getting married to a monstrous-looking girl that freakishly looked like me."

"That's a terrible dream." Leonhardt dismissed the dream and wriggled his body to be able to see Elizabeth a little better.

"That's why I hated it so much and I got so scared. I screamed over and over, trying to wake myself, and I thought that no one would come, but..." Elizabeth's cheeks were dyed the color of summer roses. Leonhardt held his breath just in case she could hear his loudly beating heart. "Leon came to save me, this time as well. Thank you."

Elizabeth placed a kiss on Leonhardt's forehead, causing him to freeze in place with Elizabeth's hair curled in his hand.

The screams he heard earlier were really because of a nightmare. Even though he was relieved that it was not because of something else, it shook him that the things that had made her suffer in the duke's residence still left some residue in her heart. He said, "It's okay. It's just a dream. How about you return to them as much as you suffered if you dream of something like that again?"

"Return?"

"Well... maybe making the duke wear piping hot shoes, or make the duchess wear a corset... Just imagine it like that?"

"B-but they're still my parents..."

Leonhardt bit his tongue. *They were still her parents.* This one sentence had once become the reason the duke and duchess of Elysium could freely go around the imperial palace until the moment she died, and it had served as an excuse for them to make a ludicrous statement of pushing the girl's younger sister to be his concubine right next door to their dying daughter.

It would've been better if she were more merciless. True to her name as an Elysium—the Descendants of Angels—she closed her eyes no matter what the duke and duchess did and took their side all because they were still, at least in name, her parents.

"I wish you were merciless instead. Just like a child who tears off a dragonfly's wings without knowing she could, it would've been better if you were pure yet cruel."

"What are you saying all of a sudden? Why would you tear off an innocent dragonfly's wings?"

"Lizzie, can you really say that they were real parents? Good parents?"

Elizabeth closed her mouth again. It was something that she never considered. They gave birth to her, fed her, raised her, and brought her to Leon. Weren't all of those enough to make them good parents?

"Back in the welcoming reception, didn't you hug them to confirm something? What did you feel back then?" Looking at Elizabeth's stiffened expression, Leonhardt clicked his tongue. It was like she was facing a mountain beyond another mountain. She couldn't even get on the cotton candy-like pink cloud called the feeling of liking someone before she had to face the dark clouds again. The only thing Leonhardt could do was advise her on how to get away from those dark clouds by herself.

"But my parents are... they..."

"Gave birth to you, raised you, and arranged an engagement with me before you were born?"

"That's why they're..."

"Raising you is the logical thing to do after giving birth to you. If they had always planned to make you the future empress before you were even born, they should've raised you even more preciously. Those are just what they are supposed to do. In fact... they don't have the right to be parents for how much they've made you suffer."

"Leonhardt!" Elizabeth's eyes widened.

Leonhardt got up from his position and held Elizabeth's shoulders firmly. "It's already late. Let's go back to sleep. If you dream of the same thing, get your revenge then. It's only a dream anyway." Leonhardt hugged Elizabeth and patted her back gently.

Their chests, pressed together in the hug, thumped with twin heartbeats.

"My heart... is racing. I can't look at Leon's face. It's strange."

"It's normally like that. That's okay."

"How does Leon know that?"

Leonhardt hugged Elizabeth tighter and buried his face in her hair. "Because... I've always been like that from the moment I saw you."

CHAPTER FORTY-SIX

That night, Elizabeth had another dream. This time, the duchess of Elysium appeared. Everyone in the welcome reception crowd wore light attire, but she wore a tight corset and heavy jewelry. The duchess offered a horrifying smile, one that appeared to rip her mouth from ear to ear, as she stretched her arms wide towards Elizabeth. Beside her, soaked in champagne, the duke mirrored the gesture, his arms also wide open for their daughter.

Elizabeth closed her eyes and thought of a rat. A small rat, the little one Mimir had summoned. The adorable rat that came out of the duchess' ridiculously huge hair—smothered with oil to fix it in place—and gave a curtsy.

After the first, another came. And another. Countless rats started to emerge from the duchess' hair. They squeaked as they held hands and began to dance in a circle around the duke and the duchess.

The whole thing made Elizabeth laugh out loud. She remembered what she had wanted to confirm that day. Just as Leonhardt had said, the only affection she had left for them was her basic gratitude for raising her. The embrace she had wanted so much, the words of love that she wanted to hear... they were merely a sweet lie, whispered into her ears for their own benefit and not for her sake.

Elizabeth woke up and fell into deep thought. She brushed through her long hair with her hand, furrowing her brows and frowning.

Even later in the morning, having been unable to sleep well all night, Elizabeth kept nodding off. She rejected Leonhardt's suggestion to take a walk outside and headed to the study instead.

It might be insignificant when compared to the library in the imperial palace, but this place was filled with interesting books she'd never seen in the imperial court. In case she fell asleep again, she set a chair right by the window with plenty of sunlight and took a soft blanket with her. She also prepared a kettle of tea and some light snacks before going around the study to find a title that stood out to her.

The book she read for starters was a romance novel. A man and a woman meeting, falling in love, suffering through conflict, overcoming that conflict together, and eventually becoming happy together—exactly Elizabeth's taste.

Seeing the pile of books that Elizabeth had already read forming a tower, the maids exchanged glances with each other. It seemed like spring had come to the young lady who hadn't had much emotion when she came to the imperial palace at ten years old.

And so, the two lived happily ever after.

Before she knew it, Elizabeth was wiping her tears. She sniffled into the handkerchief she had prepared. The deep love and conflict were too provocative for Elizabeth, who was still new to even the feeling of liking someone.

Not all romance novels ended happily. Even though the title and beginning might look happy, some of the lovers were ultimately unable to overcome the conflict and went separate ways, only able to wish each other happiness. Reading those kinds of stories made Elizabeth wonder. What the protagonist wanted most was their partner's happiness, and what the partner wanted most was them staying together—so why couldn't they?

Elizabeth opened the next book, thinking that if the main characters in the novel knew everything she knew, they would burst into tears as if the world had come crashing down.

The next book was a collection of stories handed down around the nearby sea. Even the tale that was the motif for the theater play was included, with several variations.

As Elizabeth read through the developments, she blinked curiously. *Why is it that the main characters who love each other hug and kiss?* Overall, she was still a child with an innocent curiosity. Elizabeth then tried to remember all the people who had placed a kiss on her forehead, but not one of them made her feel like her whole body was melting, or made her wish that time would stop, as was written in the story. Though her heart did race a little whenever Leonhardt treated her courteously...

Elizabeth covered herself with the blanket from head to toe, alone in the study. From that position, she stretched her hand out to the pile of books she had been reading and took out a book with a story of first love. She flipped through the pages.

Heart racing, pounding, fluttering so much they were too shy to look at each other's eyes, as well as wiggling their fingers just to touch each other because of their bashfulness. The author expressed the feelings of the young lovers treating those small moments as eternal and taking their breath away as "a lemon."

Lemon... Lemon... Leon... Elizabeth giggled as she repeated the silly pun in her head.

The story was cut short, sadly ending when the female lead became ill. Still, the young couple sharing a hurried, stolen kiss beneath sunflowers, and spending a moonlit summer night aglow in each other's love was intense.

It was a story that Elizabeth had read so many times, but she read it slowly again from the beginning. By the time she closed the last page, Elizabeth had long been sniffling. On a night when the moonlight glowed, rippling over the water, the female lead threw up blood in the male lead's arms as she trembled, like the moon on the dark waves. Her final wish was for him to make her summer an eternal summer.

Just as the female lead wished, that summer became her very last summer and a summer that would never end. No matter how many times Elizabeth read it—the male lead crying out, embracing his lover's body that had grown cold— she just sobbed.

But with this process, before she knew it, Elizabeth was getting used to the feeling of love.

"You were in the study all day today, huh?"

"Yes…"

"Your eyes are swollen. Sad stories are good, but how about reading something light and fun sometimes?" Leonhardt said gently as he stroked Elizabeth's cheek.

Elizabeth had been overlapping the faces of the male leads in the romance novels she was reading all day with Leonhardt's face, so she took a step back without realizing.

"Lizzie?"

"It's nothing. I'm okay. I guess… I just read too many books."

"Reading books is fine, but your eyes will go bad if you read too much, you know," he teased.

Elizabeth just nodded.

Although Leonhardt felt suspicious that Elizabeth seemed different from usual, he went back to his own room.

Elizabeth was left alone in the corridor. She leaned on the wall and closed her eyes. One day, just like the main characters in the novels, Leonhardt will—to me... Elizabeth's face was so red that steam rose from the top of her head. She darted off down the corridor.

Will he treat me gently like the male leads in the novel?

There were also some books that probably weren't appropriate for her age among the books she had been reading. The maids who cleaned up the things she had left behind just shrugged it off, thinking she wouldn't get it anyway. Still, they collected the borderline sensual books separately and put them somewhere she couldn't see.

In case anyone could read her thoughts, Elizabeth rushed back to her room and plopped herself down on the bed, hugging a pillow the size of her torso.

The male lead in the story had a completely different look from Leonhardt, and the female lead also had a completely different hair and eye color from Elizabeth. Yet somehow, whenever she tried to imagine their appearance in her head, the image of the two protagonists was gone, replaced by her and Leonhardt's faces.

Elizabeth kicked around the bed before lying down facing the window, trying to slowly settle her breathing.

From... from tomorrow, I need to stop reading such books... Elizabeth gave a firm nod as she made the decision.

The servants who had been taking care of the study couldn't even bask in the happiness of having a guest visit the study since Elizabeth immediately stopped going to the study just the next day. She'd never heard of there being a side effect from reading books, but she thought it was weird that she would remember the sentences of description of the protagonists whenever she looked at Leonhardt.

Elizabeth also began deliberately avoiding Leonhardt whenever she saw him to prevent her face from flushing red.

Leonhardt, who didn't know her circumstances, could only pray and pray that Elizabeth's adolescence would quickly pass.

"Lizzie."

"Y-yes?"

"Uh... father said he wanted to go fishing... do you want to come along?"

Desperate, Elizabeth mustered her strength to try to *not* remember the anecdotes of the main characters from the novels.

"Uh… you don't have to if you don't want to." Leonhardt scratched his head awkwardly and took a step back, misunderstanding the situation due to Elizabeth closing her eyes thinking nonsense thoughts.

Elizabeth wanted to tell him to wait, but the door was already closed. She went to the terrace, upset, and watched the Crown Prince and the emperor leave to enjoy themselves at the fishing grounds.

She obviously wouldn't be able to see them fish without a telescope, but Elizabeth rested her chin on the handrail and let out a sigh. Elizabeth, not knowing that the emotion she was feeling was closer to "love" than "like," felt sleepy under the warm summer sunlight. She returned to her bed to lie down.

The wind secretly visited the place Elizabeth was at through an open window, leaving a silent knock on the lace curtain.

When Elizabeth woke up after some shut-eye, it had become noisy outside. Elizabeth fixed her disheveled hair before going out. She burst into laughter seeing Leonhardt showing off a large fish.

"Even the cooks at the imperial palace hadn't been given the honor of cooking the ingredients flown over by His Majesty himself."

The people in the kitchen made idle remarks as they received the spoils of war from the emperor and the Crown Prince. Leonhardt, who still smelled fishy even after quickly washing, went up the stairs. Was it his misunderstanding that Elizabeth looked happy for him?

Elizabeth went down three stairs towards Leonhardt first, meeting him there to place a light kiss on his forehead.

"...L-Lizzie?"

"It's a reward for catching such a big fish!" Seeing Leonhardt's face flush red in an instant, Elizabeth was sure. Leonhardt liked her. And she liked Leonhardt. Otherwise, there was no way that her heart would flutter with pitapats and thrash like she was being tossed by a wave.

"...I should catch a whale next time."

"A whale?"

As Leonhardt stared at a corner of the ceiling, confused about how to explain it. He came up with a good idea, pointing at the hall on the first floor. "Do you see that fish formed by mosaics over there?"

"Yes. The one that's bigger than other fish, right?"

"That's a whale. It's probably bigger than your average sailing boat."

"How can there be a fish like that...? Leon, are you teasing me?"

"It's real! If we catch even just one whale, the port won't even need to fish for ten years."

"Hehe..." Elizabeth looked at Leonhardt, wondering which part was a bluff and which part was real. "Is that true?"

"It's true."

"Then show me next time, okay?"

"I promise you. Right, there must be an encyclopedia of fish in the study..."

Elizabeth grabbed onto Leonhardt's sleeves to stop him from going straight to the study. "Leon, you smell like the sea."

Leonhardt figured out the meaning of Elizabeth's roundabout statement and turned red again in embarrassment. "I-I'll go wash up first..."

Only then did Elizabeth let go of Leonhardt. Actually, she didn't dislike Leonhardt being basked in the smell of the sea. She was rather proud of him and thought he looked amazing for coming out victorious against such a big creature. What would it feel like to be embraced like that? Elizabeth looked down to the mosaic on the floor.

CHAPTER FORTY-SEVEN

In the middle of a small and humble celebration that was unlike anything held in the imperial palace, the people preparing for the drama festival were busy as bees. Busier, even. The workers gritted their teeth, blaming the Crown Prince who had recently visited and talked to Avon, who was in charge of everything for the drama festival, into changing the plot. The costume team, the stage design team, and the directing team especially resented Leonhardt since they had to change everything to match the new script written by Avon in a day. Even the musicians in charge of the music had to put down their instruments for a while to move heavier objects here and there to change the sets.

When Avon announced that they would have to change everything, they said it was impossible and spoke with bravado that no matter what new interpretation he was bringing, they would never change it. However, the interpretation Avon brought was unlike anything they'd seen before. It had an ending that would make both the audience and the protagonists in the story happy, unlike the existing interpretation.

The previous ones might have been a happy story for the audience, but it was a sad and sorrowful story for the protagonists. Some village natives had become tired of such plot and were impressed by the new interpretation. In the end, they submitted to Avon's pestering, the Crown Prince's imperial decree, and the greed as artists to present such a charming story on stage.

"Sir! We're ready for costume fitting!" The costume team moved busily to make new costumes, recycling the original costumes as much as possible. The stage production team was supposed to move the bubbles set pieces to the sky set originally, but they had to send them to the sea set instead. They spent hours discussing how to change the scene.

While everyone else was busy scurrying around, Avon sat, proudly smiling in the middle of the chaos.

"We're starting the dress rehearsal!"

The story, which had its ending changed all of a sudden, played out on the stage with all the actors and company watching. Once the final scene ended and they saw that the temporary theater's curtain had been lowered, everyone cheered.

They did it. Just a day before their performance, they made it!

"I've said this before, but Avon, there will be no second time. This is the first and last time."

"Why would His Highness the Crown Prince suddenly give such a story…? It's almost a miracle that the machines are working properly."

"I feel like going crazy because I keep mistaking the lines with the previous ones! What if I still make a mistake during the real thing? This time, His Majesty the Emperor and Her Majesty the Empress are also going be there!"

"Okay, everyone, focus. We are going to do fine. Let's hang in there until the end and wait for His Highness to give us a special imperial gift!"

"Just watch if he just lets it pass even though we've worked this hard. I'm going to…"

"You're going to what? Chase him off to the imperial palace with a knife like you're some pirate?"

"That wouldn't be too bad! Anyway, I won't stand still, so…"

The atmosphere from before the rehearsal had been so tense, but it was finally easing up. Avon beamed. The seed the Crown Prince had sown had bloomed into an even more beautiful flower than he expected.

People who were born in the sea would always long for the sea and slowly wither to death. It would probably be the same for the empress, Avon dared to guess. The salty wind that held her small, wriggling hands the moment she was born and the sound of waves welcoming her birth must have imprinted on her and made her return.

I heard the empress had gone through a time of hardship... Avon lifted his head to see the residence where the imperial family was staying. *May this performance let her be free from the birdcage called being an empress for even a short moment*, Avon prayed, and then he went to inspect the stage again.

Instead of going to the beach to pick up shells, Leonhardt sat beside Elizabeth, offering her chocolates shaped like seafood. Contrary to his worries that the sardine-shaped treat would let out a fishy smell, it was as sweet as any other chocolate. Unlike Leonhardt, who hesitated when it came to the sardine-shaped chocolate, Elizabeth gulped it down. Relaxing on the terrace, she nibbled on another one, looking down at her book and smiling peacefully.

"It's getting hotter. Do you want to eat the chocolates before they all melt? Or should we just share them with the servants?" Leonhardt asked, putting a hat on her after seeing that the sunlight was hitting her face.

Elizabeth noticed that his earlobes were turning red as he looked at the far horizon, so she covered her mouth with her book to hide her smile.

Leonhardt was once more relieved seeing her like that. He picked up a clam-shaped chocolate left on the table and offered it to Elizabeth. "Say ahh."

Elizabeth smiled as she opened her mouth. For hours, it seemed, Leonhardt had been personally feeding her sweets without taking a break. She told him, "It feels like I've become the protagonist of this novel I'm reading. It's a scene where she gets fed chocolates or other sweets by the person she loves while they confess their love for each other."

Leonhardt tensed his arm so as not to drop the cup he was holding. "Confess their love?"

"I like you, I love you, please be my only sweetness, as sweet as chocolate—that sort of thing."

Leonhardt felt his cheeks pointlessly blush at the lines Elizabeth cited so casually. "Do you want to eat one more chocolate? There's also a violet candy."

"Give me candy this time instead of chocolate. Anyway, what is love exactly?" Elizabeth opened her mouth. The sour and sweet lemon-flavored candy washed off the thick sweet of the chocolates. Licking the flavor from her lips, she said, "Leon, tell me you like me."

Leonhardt's heart thumped at that moment. "I-I like you, Elizabeth. Like this?"

"How much do you like me? Tell me in what way you like me, too." Elizabeth pushed, her smile full of mischief and curiosity.

Leonhardt pulled out all the vocabulary he knew and began to make a speech about how miraculous Elizabeth's existence was to him. "Just a word from you makes my heart go from heaven to hell thousands of times in a day." He took a long breath and asked, "Does that help?"

"Hmm... I think it's at least better than the books. I shall give you a chocolate as a reward. Leon, say ahh."

Leonhardt munched on the chocolate Elizabeth gave before returning to his seat.

Unlike Leonhardt, who complained that he should've brought a fishing rod, Elizabeth was satisfied with her book. This time, she was reading a collection of fairy tales for adults. Starting from the first time Elizabeth found out how many metaphors, symbolism, hidden stories, and ideas were behind fairy tales through this book, she had been reading the book over and over again throughout the summer to the point that the corners of the book had grown ragged.

She told Leonhardt, "There's the original version of the drama festival here."

"The story about the Little Mermaid?"

"Yes. It's a completely different story from the one Leon told me about, so I was a little surprised."

"Hmm..." Leonhardt responded indifferently. He had read that book before. He had been quite shocked to learn how much of the original story was adapted to protect a child's hopes and dreams.

"I wonder what it was about the Little Mermaid that made the prince fall for her? And I wonder what made the Little Mermaid like the Prince so much?"

"Love usually makes everyone go crazy."

"Not like that. This book is looking at fairy tales from a very realistic perspective."

"Then maybe because of their dubious relationship?"

"Dubious... relationship? That exists?"

Leonhardt cleared his throat when he realized that he had just made a slip of the tongue. "Like having a second wife he truly loves instead of the partner of a political marriage he didn't want... Lizzie, let's end this topic here. It's not good for children."

"I'm not a child anymore, though?"

"You are still young. Also, keep what I just said a secret. If mother found out, she'd have to lecture me and the Imperial Order of Knights."

"Why the Imperial Order of Knights ...?"

"Everything I'm not supposed to know comes from those guys."

Elizabeth tipped her head at Leonhardt's words. "We're also in a political marriage, right?"

"Since it's an arranged marriage before birth... I guess so?"

"Is this a marriage you don't want?"

"No way. Haven't I told you earlier just how much I like you, Elizabeth?"

"Then you won't get a second wife, right? Her Majesty said that it'll be better for the empire to have more successors. And to do that..."

"Stop, stop! Stop right there. What has mother been teaching you exactly? Lizzie, as long as you're with me, I will never, ever! Even if heaven collapses, I will never look at another woman, so don't worry."

"Can I trust you? The men that Her Majesty talked about always..."

"I swear! I swear on everything, this Leonhardt Tristan von Esphedor's heart, mind, and soul will only belong to Elizabeth Isolde von Elysium."

Hearing that, Elizabeth buried her body deep into her chair, looking somewhat relieved. She mumbled, "I want a macaron."

Leonhardt sat up and popped a raspberry macaron into Elizabeth's mouth.

"Leon, have you ever dreamed of me?" Elizabeth put down her book. It might have been a nightmare, but she did dream of him once.

"Me? You appearing in my dream? Uh… so…" Leonhardt did a double take and covered his mouth with both hands.

A thin line appeared in between Elizabeth's brows. "What kind of dream was it?"

Leonhardt just shook his head. It was a dream that he couldn't tell her, who was so pure, innocent, and knew nothing. Someone who would be immediately tainted the moment he touched her.

"But I told you mine. It's not fair."

Leonhardt still shook his head, as if he couldn't say it even if he died.

"Wh-why do you suddenly want to know about that…? You've appeared in my dreams. Of course, you have. A few times even."

"Then why can't you tell me what they were about?"

"That's… so… uh…"

"Was it a dream of you eating delicious food by yourself behind my back? If it's like that, then I forgive you. In return, give me one more chocolate."

Leonhardt unwrapped the chocolate in a hurry before putting it into Elizabeth's mouth, muttering, "It's especially hot today…"

"Don't go off-topic! Tell me already, please?"

Leonhardt exercised the right to remain silent until the end, for Lady Elizabeth's honor and innocence.

This is all because… because of this damn young body! It was unbelievable that he had to endure the tediousness of puberty twice. Leonhardt blocked Elizabeth's mouth with sweet snacks as his heart ached. He said, "Anyway! Tomorrow is finally the drama festival."

"See, you're changing the topic again. The drama festival…"

"The drama festival is held every year, so let's come see it again next year. And then the next year, and then the next year. Okay?"

"Really?"

"Since the story was written for mother this time, I'll write a story for you next time, Elizabeth," he promised.

"Are you going to tell me the ending in advance?" she asked.

"That's not it…!"

"Can you promise?" Elizabeth held out her little finger. Leonhardt then linked it with his own. "We'll come to the drama festival every year. This is a promise, Your Highness the Crown Prince.”

“I promise you, Elizabeth.”

A STORMING BEACH

CHAPTER
FORTY-EIGHT

The seagulls, who made little waves with every flap of their wings, had disappeared without a trace. The seasoned sailors clicked their tongues when they saw the shape of the clouds and pulled their ships to harbor.

Avon, writing a story in the sand, also looked up at the sky with an uneasy expression.

"Today's weather is so lovely!" Elizabeth exclaimed.

"Going to be a storm."

"Storm?" Elizabeth was upset, unsure why they couldn't go out when the place where the skies and the seas met was so bright.

Leonhardt spoke indifferently as he turned over the papers that had become soggy from the moisture in the air. "It's always calm before the storms."

Elizabeth grimaced, unconvinced of what he said.

Meanwhile, the empress was having a hard time even smelling something from the sea. The maids checked her food over and over to ensure the dishes served to her included as little seafood as possible.

"Even though I came back to my hometown after so long... Your Majesty, you know how tasty it is to eat a fresh oyster with a squeeze of lemon juice."

"Of course, but Empress, I'm worried that you might not even be able to eat grilled abalones with butter in your state, let alone an oyster."

"*Huff*... We can come back here before I die, right?"

"What ominous thing are you saying? Let's come back here next year, and the year after that. Who knows, maybe the quality of the seafood would get even better by then," the emperor told his wife. "Both shrimp and clams must have plenty of food so they can be plump..." Realizing late his slip of the tongue, the emperor winced awkwardly.

"By the way, it looks like a storm is coming."

"A storm?"

"I can tell by the shape of the clouds. I hope there won't be any damage..."

"Huh... Even though tomorrow is the drama festival already..."

As the empress leaned back on the bed to look out the window, the emperor, beside her, patted her hand worriedly.

A small drop of rain finally fell on the vast ocean. The single raindrop that melted into the sea without a trace quickly became a heavy downpour that ripped through the sky and pierced the water like needles.

"It really is a rainstorm…"

"See?"

"How did you know?"

"I can tell from the shape of the clouds. And didn't you see that the seagulls have disappeared?"

"Hmmm…"

"The rain will come in. Just in case, it would be better to close the curtains as well."

"Even the curtains?"

Leonhardt closed the glass door to the terrace and elaborately closed the curtains. At a glance, the sea looked like it was raging. The winds seized the poster of the drama festival and threw it through the air. "If we're unlucky, we might even greet a fish a good morning on the terrace tomorrow."

If they were really unlucky—never mind the drama festival—it would even be difficult for them to make their way back to the imperial palace. The news that the drama festival had been postponed came to Elizabeth and Leonhardt before it was time for afternoon tea. The locals said it was an unprecedented storm and tried to console them by saying it was Manannán, the God of the Sea, welcoming His Majesty the Emperor in his own way.

As she watched the rain beating down on the windows, Elizabeth thought it looked like a bucket of water being poured from the roof.

"Now that I think about it, speaking of a mansion by the sea under the rain... One story comes to mind..."

"Leon?"

Leonhardt twirled the teaspoon in the teacup as he lifted his gaze.

"...Want to hear?"

Rumble... Bang!

Lightning flashed behind him. Elizabeth nodded even though her shoulders cowered. A corner of her heart began to race. The story Leonhardt told was about a hidden secret of some mansion.

"Once upon a time... there was a large mansion on a cliff along the coast, where ships too often crashed against the unforgiving rocks and sunk into the sea..."

A large mansion on a cliff along the coast, where ships often capsized due to the large number of rocks. The lights in the mansion were never turned off to make it serve as a lighthouse. Whenever a ship got run aground by the storms, the person who would run out first to rescue them would be the good-natured, praiseworthy man who was the lord of the mansion. However, there was a strangely gloomy and bleak energy always hovering inside the mansion.

"One day, a young lady came to that mansion. She came as none other than the landlady of the mansion."

"And then?" Elizabeth had wrapped herself in a blanket. She clutched it closer, gazing intently at Leonhardt as he continued.

"But the servants in that mansion acted as if that lady was invisible. Even though they should've devoted themselves to her and politely treated her as the mansion's landlady... they were all cold and ignored her existence the best that they could, as if they were treating her as a doll. The head maid, in particular, would stop walking and glare at her with eyes wide open whenever she saw the lady pass through the hallway. Only after the lady cleared her throat in discomfort did the head maid greet her and pass by."

"Wh-why? That lady didn't do anything wrong."

Leonhardt spread his eyes wide and impersonated the head maid in the story.

"However, that mansion's friendly lord and the servants were actually hiding a terrible secret!"

"Eek!" Elizabeth yanked the blanket up to cover her eyes.

"What was that secret...?" Elizabeth asked, trembling as her blue eyes peeked out from the blanket.

Leonhardt slowly leaned towards Elizabeth. Behind him, the sky was full of dark clouds as if thick black ink had been spilled all across it. The thunder roared ceaselessly. And he whispered into her ear under his breath... "It was..."

"My sweethearts!"

"Kyaaah!"

"Eli-Elizabe... Lizzie! You're choking me...! Mother?" The moment Leonhardt was going to say the secret of the mansion in a mischievous voice, the door had opened with a bang. Elizabeth, who had been holding onto Leonhardt's arm in nervousness, was scared to her wits and clung to Leonhardt's neck.

Leonhardt just wanted to tease her a little, but he ended up having to risk his life in exchange. As he glared at the empress, she looked alternatively at the two teenagers on the bed. She asked, "...did I interrupt you kids?"

"Something good?"

"Mother, do you feel well?" Leonhardt switched the topic as he carefully pried away the pile of blankets covering Elizabeth's face, one by one.

The empress nodded. She still felt like throwing up, but she always wanted to move around whenever she felt like that. "What are you having so much fun talking about?"

"His Highness was telling me about a mysterious mansion with secrets."

"Oh my? Could that story be... What good timing! I happen to have brought something fun since you might be bored because of the storms."

With a gesture by the empress, Elizabeth and Leonhardt got off the bed and sat in front of the table. "If we're talking about secrets, this mansion also has a lot. They are the things that me and my brothers hid during our childhood without the servants and maids knowing. I was going to clear them all up before I left for the imperial palace back then... but I couldn't find the last item at all... If you're okay with it, can you find it for me?"

"Do we have a lead?"

"This entire mansion is the lead. Come to think of it, I hid it when I was around Elizabeth's age, so you might be able to find it soon!" the empress beamed with a clap.

Elizabeth had gotten out of the blanket and was listening intently to the empress' words. Leonhardt looked up at his mother and tried to smile.

And so, Elizabeth and Leonhardt began to explore the mansion with only one lamp in hand. Just as the empress said, they found various traces that would have been difficult to find if they didn't have an eye level equal to Elizabeth's.

"Look at this, Leon. I thought it was a wallpaper, but it was actually a drawing of a wallpaper in place of a torn piece!"

"I guess mother's drawing skills have been outstanding since she was this age."

The drawing resembled an exquisite wallpaper pattern so closely that one might not recognize it as a drawing at first glance. However, upon closer inspection, it became clear that the color of that particular section was different.

Leonhardt expressed his admiration for Elizabeth's observation before heading to the next room.

"This is..."

"Is it a room for men?"

"I guess so. The navy... This seems to be the room of the one who would've been my maternal uncle if he were alive."

"Come to think of it, Leon also doesn't have relatives, right?"

"Hm... now that you say it, that's true. I think there are some collateral nobles here and there since we are the imperial family, but I don't really remember ever meeting a relative."

"Then both Leon and I would be all alone when our parents pass away."

"Why are you suddenly saying such a thing...?"

Elizabeth had been so bothered by her recent dream that an uneasy expression overtook her as she looked out the window. It was completely dark outside.

"Lizzie!" When Leonhardt discovered that Elizabeth was opening the window, he blocked her with his body in a hurry.

"It's easy to get swept to the sea on days like this. Be careful."

"Swept... to the sea...?"

"The sea is basically the eternal graveyard for the sailors."

Elizabeth gasped. "Don't say such a scary thing! Kyaaah!" Elizabeth backed away from the window at once. Just then, along with a loud boom, a light flashed so fiercely that it banished the darkness for a brief moment.

"Lizzie, Lizzie? Are you okay?"

Elizabeth was closing her eyes tight and covering her ears. Leonhardt, pinned under her, didn't know what else to do other than to raise his hand and press them against the back of Elizabeth's.

"Can you not hear them now?" *Oh, she obviously can't hear me since I'm covering her ears.* Leonhardt just waited until Elizabeth opened her eyes.

"Sorry!" Fortunately, Elizabeth quickly realized who she was pinning down and moved away in a hurry.

"What now, should we keep looking?"

"Umm..."

"If you are too scared and want to stop, I'm okay with it."

"I... I'm not scared!"

"...Really?"

Elizabeth nodded. She didn't want to give up here. Leonhardt respected her opinion.

Still, Elizabeth gripped Leonhardt's hand very tightly as she moved to the next room with shaky steps. She howled, "It's a ghooooost!"

"Lizzie! D-don't choke me!"

The moment they opened the door, something fell from the ceiling. Elizabeth grabbed Leonhardt's necktie so hard she seemed to dangle from it. Leonhardt shone a light from the lamp onto the fallen object. Instinctively, he moved backward. "Th... that's..."

"I've read stories about how corpses from the sea get revived! I'm sure it's that!" she murmured.

"Lizzie, calm down, relax now... This room's owner... doesn't seem like he had a very good hobby." Leonhardt reached out and tapped on the thing that had fallen in front of the door with his foot.

"A skeleton... There's a skeleton... a skeleton..." Elizabeth muttered, out of her mind.

"Yup. A skeleton it is. Though it's just a doll made of black cloth roughly painted. They were probably planning on surprising the person entering this room to clean up."

"...A doll?"

Leonhardt nodded as he directed the light onto the black doll that had fallen at Elizabeth's feet. Just in case the skeleton might cackle around by itself, she approached it slowly, trembling. The doll under the light was covered in plenty of dust.

"So, it was really a doll..." Elizabeth said as she hid behind him, who was fiddling with the skeleton-drawn doll nonchalantly.

"Lizzie, are you really okay?"

Elizabeth nodded from behind his back. Just like the other time when she once stood behind him, Leonhardt's back felt strong, safe, reliable enough for her protection.

CHAPTER
FORTY-NINE

Leonhardt grabbed Elizabeth's hand tightly as they began to explore the room in earnest. The whole room was a mess, as if hoping for its owner to come back soon. An open book collected dust so thick it served as a bookmark. When they blew off the dust, they could see that it was an illustrated saga of sailors.

"That thing on the wall... it must be that, right?"

"Why is the key used to steer a ship on the wall...? This room's owner must've really liked ships."

Elizabeth stepped cautiously, still clinging to Leonhardt, as if she were walking on a wobbling, capsizing ship. She felt like a large, shriveled hand might emerge any moment from under the bed and grab her ankle.

"Is it the room of one of mother's brothers?"

"Hmmm... I don't think so." Elizabeth counted something with her hand before shaking her head. The number of rooms they had found so far equaled the number of brothers the empress had. It meant the owner of this room was either the empress herself or a guest who had been staying for a long period...

"There's a sketchbook here."

"Sketchbook?"

Elizabeth looked at Leonhardt like she was asking for permission. Instead of giving her one, Leonhardt just immediately flipped the sketchbook's pages. Line practice, spheres, cubes, and tetrahedrons filled the first several pages. After that, there were still-life drawings done clumsily with watercolors.

"The signature... is not there, huh?"

"Yes..." Elizabeth nodded. The person who painted the still-life didn't seem to know much about how to use a brush. But somehow, she felt like she'd seen this style of painting before.

"It's mother's family," Leonhardt said in a low voice as he flipped through the thick sketchbook at a high speed. Inside, a drawing that had turned yellow: some boys smiling and holding hands with each other. Starting from the oldest brother who looked more like a parent to the youngest one who was wearing a navy uniform.

"I don't see Her Majesty here...?"

"Seems like mother was too focused on drawing that she forgot to leave a space for herself."

On the next page, Leonhardt found the empress' self-portrait. She probably put her face somewhere else because she didn't want to ruin the composition.

"Everyone looks happy..." Elizabeth carefully hovered her hand over the paper to stroke it midair so as not to smudge it.

"Mother... has never talked much about her family. I learned about them through the maids and history books instead." Leonhardt's throat tightened. When he once got curious about his lineage during his childhood, Leonhardt had gone to the empress. Rather than telling him, the empress gave a lonely smile and offered him a book. Inside were details regarding the empress' family.

The noble family that resided on the most beautiful beach in the empire was a free and lively family, and they had produced outstanding navy sailors for generations. However, children who suffered from a bleeding disease were sometimes born in that family. The people murmured that it was because they made a deal with Manannán, the God of the Sea, when the First Head established the land.

After some time had passed and medical science had advanced, it was revealed that the disease was hemophilia. The people calmed down since it was also revealed that Leonhardt didn't have the disease in question, but it was once heatedly debated that the empress must be deposed from her position.

In reality, some of these people have died from that disease... Leonhardt thought as he looked at a boy who looked particularly pale in the drawing. "If these people had been alive... would I have been less lonely?"

Elizabeth leaned her head on Leonhardt's shoulder while they examined the drawing together. She had had to memorize the genealogy from her father's side, know which noble generation had Elysium blood, and all sorts of details as the lady of the house—even if she didn't want to. But she never knew much about her mother's side of the family.

"Were you lonely?"

"I... think so. Whenever the elderly retainers mentioned their granddaughters, I would imagine what it would feel like to have grandparents."

However, such thoughts completely vanished when he saw his grandparents from the history books and the portraits hanging in the imperial palace. Leonhardt told Elizabeth about how he once went in front of the portrait of the person who would've been his grandmother and yelled that he hated her with his short tongue all because he'd read about how strict and cold she was to his mother, who had been the Crown Princess at that time.

"Did you really do that?"

"For some reason, there was someone among the portraits who had exceptionally big and sharp eyes and looked so curt that it would freeze me in place whenever I saw her. If such a person were my grandmother, maybe I would've choked and died early."

Elizabeth giggled, and the sound was like a chiming bell. Yelling at his grandmother's portrait was pretty typical of the five-year-old him—the one in the empress' sketchbook. A child who wouldn't do things he was told to do and do things he wasn't supposed to do all because of his stubbornness.

"But I wonder why Her Majesty's room is this mess… I mean, I wonder why they left it as if it was waiting for her to come back soon?"

The blanket on the bed was even lumped into a ball.

"Waiting for her to come back… wouldn't it be exactly as you said?"

"Huh?"

"Apparently, grandmother was very… umm… disapproving of mother. Maybe she left the room as it is because she might come back if she can't take it anymore… That's how it was written in the book."

"Did Her Majesty really say that?" Elizabeth's eyes opened wide. Compared to the current empress' gentle and benevolent nature, those words and behavior seemed way too different.

"Well… mother fortunately kept staying in the imperial palace, but this room… maybe the servants left it on purpose so that mother can forget all the bad things whenever she decides to come back?"

"On purpose…"

Leonhardt squeezed Elizabeth's hand. All the men that had been going to inherit the family lost their lives in the sea and returned to Manannán's arms, as if they all were destined to. The brothers suffering from hemophilia also all passed away before they turned ten. However, it had become too ambiguous to give the title of the duke to someone from a collateral family who had already become the head of another family. And that was how the empress' family ended up relegated to the pages of history books.

"…Will the Elysium family turn out like that, too?"

"Lizzie?"

"I'm an only child… I don't have a suitable relative either… Will our family also end as it is?"

I wish they would naturally disappear like that. Still, Leonhardt comforted Elizabeth, who might still have some affection for her family left, as he began to jump in place to search for a hidden pattern between the wallpapers or a part of the floor that might give a weirdly different sound when he stepped on it. "Lizzie—what do—you wish—would happen?"

He had been stepping and jumping on various spots on the dark blue rug, but he couldn't hear the unique sound that would come out if there were an empty space underneath.

"...I don't know." Elizabeth looked at the titles of the various adventure stories and travel books on the shelf before shaking her head.

"If your family ends with you, doesn't that mean that there will be no more ladies who will have to go through empress lessons or bride lessons the way you did?" Leonhardt pretended not to know as he glanced at Elizabeth from the corner of his eyes and checked under the bed.

Nothing there either. Leonhardt swept the dust from his head, coughing as he checked on Elizabeth's reaction.

"...Is that so...?"

"Though of course, the next generation's duke of Elysium—if they get one. In the case that there is one, they might not necessarily turn out to be like... your parents."

Elizabeth fell into deep thought as she studied the ornaments on the wall. After hearing what Leonhardt said, she thought that it might be possible. However, the thought of a family that had been part of the empire's history disappearing was somehow saddening.

"The empire's very first empress was also from Elysium, wasn't she?"

"Was she? Oh, I guess so. Isabella... I don't remember her middle name."

"I wonder if she was raised like me?"

"Would they really be like that from the start?"

"Right...? Then how did it..."

How did it turn out like this? Elizabeth lowered her head, unable to continue her words... *Huh?* There was a golden reflection on her shoe's sleek toecap. Elizabeth raised her head and searched for what was shining gold.

"...I guess Her Majesty really liked stories about the sea, the pirates, and the sailors." Behind the skeleton that had scared her out of her wits earlier, there was a pair of cutlass swords crossed on the wall.

Leonhardt tried to reassure Elizabeth that they were probably given as a present to her by her brothers, who were in the navy. "It's strangely crooked. Mother is someone who can't bear something like that, you see. Could it be heavier on one side?"

Leonhardt stood on tiptoe to try to fix the crooked ornament. However, he couldn't reach it. Elizabeth also tried to hop and stretch out her arms, but she couldn't reach the ornament either.

Leonhardt prompted, "Lizzie, get on my back."

Leonhardt put his knees and hands on the floor without hesitation to turn himself into a foothold. Looking at Leonhardt's action flustered Elizabeth. "There's a perfectly fine chair there so why...?"

"We can't mess with that chair now, can we?"

"Then aren't we supposed to not mess with this ornament as well?"

"Well, this might be the item that mother asked us to find!"

Even so, Elizabeth hesitated to step on Leonhardt's back. He was her fiancé, the Crown Prince, and the person she liked. For some reason, she felt so apologetic and shy that she couldn't move her feet as she wanted like earlier.

"Or do you want to ride on my shoulders?" Leonhardt said as he looked to the side. "If you don't want that either... should I just carry you on my back?"

Elizabeth then finally nodded at that.

Leonhardt carried Elizabeth on his back with ease and approached the wall. "How is it? Can you grab anything?"

"Mmm... Oh, I can!"

"Did you get it?"

"I got it...! Huh? Leon, there's a hole here. There... seems to be something inside the hole?"

"What?"

When she pushed the ornament forward, there was a hole that was obviously manmade with sparkly things inside it.

"Maybe these items are what mother was talking about?"

"Is that so...? Kyaaah!"

Leonhardt tensed so that Elizabeth, who staggered backwards, wouldn't fall down. Elizabeth tried to put her arm inside the hole, but she screamed and shrieked at touching something unthinkable.

"Isn't this... a gun?"

"Why is a gun here?"

"Why was mother holding something like this?" Leonhardt tapped the gun—old and wrapped in spider webs on the floor—with his feet.

"...Umm, Leon."

"Yes?"

As Elizabeth examined the gun from atop Leonhardt's back, she realized the state they were in and blushed.

"...Can you let me down now?"

Leonhardt blinked a few times, then, surprised as he belatedly recognized their position, he let her get down.

CHAPTER
FIFTY

Along with the gun, Elizabeth pulled from the hole a red coral in the shape of an antler, a glass bead filled with silvery powder, and a small toy sword.

"It's still unbelievable even seeing it for myself."

"Me too."

Elizabeth and Leonhardt shared their thoughts as they put their loots on the ground. For items owned by the empress—no, by a noble family's daughter, the toys were much too simple and insignificant. Why did mother make this wall and hide these toys inside it?

"For now, we need to go get mother here. Lizzie, wait here... I get it. Let's go together." The moment Leonhardt's eyes met Elizabeth's, which seemed to express a resentful *"Are you thinking of leaving me alone here?"* with her gaze, he grinned and helped her up.

"So, you've found the treasure!" The empress, lying on her bed, smiled brightly when the two of them came in with their arms full.

"Where did you find it?"

"Umm... inside the wall... of the room you used to use, mother," Leonhardt answered with a shrinking voice.

The empress just blinked a few times at his answer. After she realized what it meant, she grabbed the cushion from her side and covered her face with it.

"Empress?"

"Mother?"

The emperor and Leonhardt ran over in alarm.

"That room... that room was the last room I slept in before I went to the imperial palace..." They couldn't hear it clearly because it was muffled by the cushion, but the empress' voice sounded like she was in tears.

The day before she left for the imperial palace, the empress put every little thing with a precious memory shared with her brothers inside that secret place. The coral that her eldest brother gave her from a trip on a trade ship. The glass bead that her sickly brother put in her hand just before he passed away. The toy sword that her mischievous elder brother, who had the least age difference with her, gave to her to say that she should just be a knight instead if she ever wanted to quit being the Crown Princess. And...

"Freyja..." the emperor called out her name in a low voice after lifting the white blanket and seeing the pistol. What was she thinking putting a pistol, a loaded one at that, into that place? Was she thinking of going back to her hometown and using the gun if she couldn't endure life in the imperial palace anymore? In his anxiety and worry, a crease lined the emperor's forehead.

"...It's an item I don't need anymore." The empress lifted her face from the cushion to don a small smile.

Both the emperor and Leonhardt found the word "anymore" slightly disturbing, yet they were still able to breathe a sigh of relief.

Meanwhile, Elizabeth was observing the gun with her hands folded behind her. She felt intense curiosity and interest at seeing one for the first time. A weapon faster, lighter, and more capable of leaving a dreadful wound compared to a sword. She said, "Umm... Your Majesty the Empress."

"What's wrong, dear?"

Even though Elizabeth thought that it was impossible, she asked the empress anyway. "Can I have this gun?"

Leonhardt's heart sank in an instant. However, he couldn't let himself grab his fiancée's shoulder in fright, to question what she meant, especially in front of his parents. It was the empress' and emperor's duty to question her.

"Can I... ask why?"

Elizabeth lowered her head and just nibbled on her lips for a while.

"Lizzie..." Leonhardt also only stared at the corners of the floor in restlessness and anxiety. No way Elizabeth wanted to have the gun for the same reason as the empress, right?

At last Elizabeth said, "I want to protect His Highness."

What came out of Elizabeth's mouth was something that he never expected. "Me?"

Leonhardt pointed at himself.

Elizabeth gave a confident nod. "When we saw the fireworks... the night His Highness became a sword master, I was not able to do anything at all. If those people had another idea, I would... I would be... I am even unable to protect myself... and I am so furious at that... furious, and also sad..." Elizabeth herself also didn't know what she was saying right now. Her speech was turning into murmured rambling, but the emperor and the empress seemed to understand what she meant. It was natural to want to protect the person she loved. It was rather a mindset that should be deemed praiseworthy than make her get scolded. In spite of that, Elizabeth was still too young.

The empress gestured for Elizabeth to come closer. Elizabeth approached her with a nervous heart.

"Do you want to protect the Crown Prince?"

"I want to provide protection to His Highness. I want to protect my own body. I do not want to be a burden to His Highness."

"How admirable." The empress smiled at Elizabeth's ambitious words. She placed a little kiss on the girl's forehead. She continued, "However, Elizabeth, a gun is a very dangerous item."

"I... I guess it is." *As expected, it won't work.* Elizabeth tried her hardest to hide her disappointment.

"That's why. Why don't you learn it when you grow up a little more? This empress will teach you herself."

"Huh?"

"Empress!"

"Mother!"

The empress waved her hand to calm the two people who were apparently so shocked at her proposition. "Just because we are women, we can't always just bite on our tongues in the face of crisis against our virtue, become a hostage and hold our allies back, or be a burden. I couldn't agree more with Elizabeth."

"But what danger can even befall a child who would be the empress of a nation?"

The empress stared scrutinizingly at the emperor. It was as if she was saying, *"Do you really not know?"*

"Ahem, ahem. It wouldn't be too bad to be able to protect one's own body at least."

Only then did the empress smile again.

"We must take all of these items to the imperial palace. That will be fine, won't it?"

"Don't you already know that if I could, I would have moved the entire sea in front of the imperial palace as well?" At the emperor's sweet words, the empress laughed and leaned her body onto his firm embrace.

"Oh right, come to think of it, I should give my sweethearts a nice reward for finding the treasure in my place."

"You are so correct, Empress. Do you two have anything you want?"

Elizabeth and Leonhardt exchanged looks with each other. In the current state of being forbidden to go out, there was only one thing they wanted.

"Please allow us to go out."

"Please grant us your imperial permission. Please—?" Elizabeth even pursed her lips and stretched the end of her words.

The emperor and empress let out a hearty laugh and nodded as if they had lost a bet.

They were going to have to return to the imperial palace immediately after the postponed drama festival was over, so making them stay only inside the mansion would be too harsh on them.

"Hurray!" Leonhardt clapped his hands with Elizabeth's as he shouted his cheers.

"We were planning to go to the lighthouse once the rain stopped. Do the Crown Prince and Elizabeth want to come along?"

Before they knew it, the rain had started to slow down. The empress forecasted that maybe, at least, it would be sunny tomorrow. But Elizabeth noticed that Leonhardt's face had gone stiff at the word lighthouse. *Leon...?*

Leonhardt's violet eyes seemed to tremble as he said, "Mother... the lighthouse is on a cliff... so it'll be dangerous..."

"What is there to worry about when His Majesty will be with us?"

I'm worried that the very His Majesty would be giving you freedom disguised as death as a present. Leonhardt's lips twitched, and his face turned pale.

"Crown Prince?" The empress sensed something was wrong.

Leonhardt gasped, coming to his senses with a shake of his head. "No... it's nothing. I'm just worried since mother has been low in spirit as of lately..."

"It is just the summer heat getting to me. I also have a plan to call a doctor already, so don't worry too much and just prepare yourself to show Elizabeth the most beautiful sight in the world tomorrow, Crown Prince."

Being told to leave in a roundabout way, Leonhardt and Elizabeth had to quietly withdraw.

"Leon... you seem very concerned." Elizabeth pressed the back of her hand against Leonhardt's cheek. "Are you not feeling well?"

Leonhardt's face was pale, and his hands were trembling. "Lizzie."

"I'm listening."

Leonhardt looked at Elizabeth with a desperate gaze, as if he was a believer who was looking for salvation from his god. He said slowly, "If... Elizabeth... if you ever wish to die... and I know your wish... will I have to kill you with my own hands?"

"L-Leon?"

"Is that the only way to release mother from the birdcage? Is there no other way? Is the future impossible to change? What Mimis Brunnr said that day, what does it really mean? Lizzie, Lizzie... I'm scared."

"What are you so scared of...?"

Leonhardt pulled Elizabeth into an embrace. Elizabeth's eyes widened, and she immediately looked around in case there was anyone passing by to see them in this state. She could hear a beating heart through the layers of their clothes.

"Of the possibility that I might lose the person I love again. Of being unable to keep my promise even though I promised time and again that I would make you happy. I'm scared of that. I feel sorry for the people who have to have an emperor who can't even protect his loved one's smile, and I also feel sorry for my future self who has to fall into despair, so I... so I..."

"Your Highness the Crown Prince Leonhardt Tristan von Esphedor." Elizabeth took Leonhardt's face with both hands to stop him from muttering incoherent words.

A shine barely returned to the purple eyes that had lost their light earlier. Elizabeth smiled. "It's okay. Leon will be just fine. I don't really know what you're so scared of, but... if it's Leon, you can do it. And if I stay by Leon's side, it'll always... always..."

"Lizzie, are you certain that you'll be happy by my side?" Leonhardt implored.

Elizabeth then pressed their foreheads together and nodded. "Didn't Leon say that you will make me happy? So, it's okay. It'll be okay. I believe in Leon."

Hearing that, Leonhardt could finally calm down a little and see ahead. Elizabeth stayed quietly in his arms, patting his back and saying everything would be fine. Leonhardt took a deep breath, his forehead buried in Elizabeth's nape, which seemed to emit all kinds of clear and pure scents like lilies of the valley, daffodils, and lotuses. For a second, Elizabeth was so nervous she held her breath. This was the first time he ever acted like this with her. However, Leonhardt only breathed a few times in that position before letting her go again.

He scratched his cheek and his ears reddened as he said he had been discourteous. Even if Elizabeth didn't understand what had just happened, her heart was racing, and she could feel her cheek warming when she pressed the back of her hand against it.

"Thanks, Lizzie."

"I didn't do anything…"

Leonhardt took Elizabeth's hand and grinned.

Today's weather was so bad that they couldn't even light up the fireworks and had to make the candles in the corridor brighter—so how come it was looking like the sun was shining bright from behind Leonhardt's face?

"Shall we rest early? The sunrise and sunset in the sea is really beautiful, you know. I really want to show it to you, Lizzie."

"Leon, have you been to the sea before?"

"Huh?"

Elizabeth tilted her head and pointed out something that had been bothering her. "You said it's your first time going to the sea, but you speak like you're quite familiar with it."

Leonhardt took a double take and bit his tongue. However, Elizabeth didn't seem to want to press it further as she just bid him good night and returned to her room. As Leonhardt was left alone in the corridor, he kept repeating to himself to exercise caution, just as Mimis Brunnr had warned him.

WIND UP THE CLOCK AGAIN

CHAPTER
FIFTY-ONE

Just as the empress had said, the raging dark clouds settled gradually into mild rain. The seagulls came back with the sun at dawn. Their wings drew shadows over the waves. The sailors exalted Manannán's name as they unwound the thick knots they had tied and sent their boats back to sea.

It was a fine day when the skies and the sea met and reflected the light. While everyone was basking in the white sunlight that formed a rainbow over the window, Leonhardt had a serious expression, like a sailor still moving through a storm.

"Leon, what's wrong...?" Because they were now allowed to go out again, Elizabeth had woken up early to get ready. She waved her hand in front of Leonhardt's hardened face.

"Uh... mmm... it's nothing," Leonhardt said, his eyes fixed on the emperor and the empress, who were discussing when they should go to the lighthouse.

"The evening would be better, wouldn't it?"

Could he stop them from going? He wanted to urge them against going to the lighthouse and walking on the rocky cliff that evening. All he could do was follow her, along with Elizabeth, and coax the empress out of any dangerous thoughts.

"Their Majesties said we're all going to go to the lighthouse to see the sunset after dinner! I'm already looking forward to it. Apparently, on days like today, the setting sun will look especially colorful and clear."

Elizabeth's words, which he would usually listen to with pleasure, didn't even register in his ears. *What if mother ends up throwing everything away in a place where Elizabeth could see? Should I just make Elizabeth stay here?* But when Leonhardt saw the girl dancing and swaying as she walked excitedly, he couldn't say anything... *We'll do everything we can. No way... no way mother will... It won't happen... It definitely... won't happen...*

Elizabeth's wish to go to the lighthouse and see the setting sun seemed to be a little stronger than Leonhardt's wish for time to pass twice as slowly as usual. Before he knew it, the emperor and the empress had changed into light outing clothes after finishing their early dinner.

The inside of his head was a disaster. Leonhardt didn't even realize that he had inserted a button into the wrong hole as he dressed. He just had to think of a way to save his mother.

"Leon, your buttons are messed up," Elizabeth said. He had always maintained the neat, prideful, and elegant attitude of a Crown Prince, but now half of his shirt was tucked into his pants while the other half hung out, and his buttons were in disarray.

Before anyone could see, Elizabeth dragged him into the room and pushed him to the door. "Seriously, Leon, do you know that you've been strange for the whole day since the morning? Suddenly asking if there was a fence around the lighthouse, insisting that you want to go there first by yourself…"

"Did… I…?"

Look at this guy? Elizabeth looked up at Leonhardt, astonished. The Crown Prince before her seemed as though half his spirit had already departed. His expression was far-gone and vacant. Elizabeth was trying to adjust Leonhardt's outfit. Then, she tapped Leon's cheeks with her small hand, only enough to bring him to his senses. "Get yourself together. I don't have anyone else but Leon to protect me if I slipped because I get blinded by the sunset."

Hearing that, Leonhardt's eyes, which had lost their spark, shook. "That's right…"

"Huh? What's right?" Elizabeth raised her head, which had been lowered to adjust Leonhardt's messy buttons.

Leonhardt pulled Elizabeth into a tight hug.
"L-Leon…?"

With his shirt half-unbuttoned and his bare chest exposed, Leonhardt held Elizabeth in his arms and inhaled her scent. Only then did all the thoughts that had been echoing in his head all day slowly begin to settle down. "You're right, Lizzie."

Elizabeth, hugged by Leonhardt in an unguarded moment, stayed frozen. As Leonhardt moved, the scent he exuded seemed to envelop her, binding like shackles around her ankles. After spending a few days in a house near the sea, instead of the mint-scented soap he usually used, he was exuding the scent of the slightly fishy and salty sea so thick she felt like she could grab it if she reached out.

"It's okay. I'll protect everyone this time."

"Everyone? Everyone, you say?"

"Elizabeth, mother, father, your future, my future, and your happiness. I'll protect them all at all costs."

Elizabeth was so distracted by the scent of sea exuding from his body, binding and paralyzing her that she couldn't understand what he was talking about. Her heart began to pound so hard it hurt.

Leonhardt hugged her as if he was an injured beast looking for a space between the rocks, but now he had become a reliable port embracing her. *Was this the scent of the perfume Elizabeth usually uses?* Leonhardt thought as he buried his face into the nape of her neck and slowly inhaled.

The scent had the mysterious power of erasing all of his anxious thoughts.

If he could, he wanted to stay like this forever. *Why didn't I notice how precious she was back then? Why did I never thank the person who would accept, embrace, and comfort me even if she didn't know what's going on?* His regrets from the future-turned-past that had faded were now swarming back in like a rising tide. Leonhardt let her go with the best smile he could make.

"Are you okay?" Elizabeth checked Leonhardt's face first and foremost. Even if she didn't know what changed in his heart, his buttons were inserted correctly now, and he had returned to the usual Leonhardt. Unbeknownst to Leonhardt, Elizabeth breathed a sigh of relief and adjusted her collar before they stepped out together.

However, for some reason, the maids, the servants, and the emperor and the empress were making a strange expression. Leonhardt and Elizabeth were puzzled by their pleased smiles, ones that looked as if they understood everything. They then realized what just went on earlier, when they were leaning on the door, and quickly let go of each other's hands.

"Ahem, ahem... S-shall we go?" Leonhardt kept clearing his throat. He offered his hand to escort her as a lady, instead of holding her hand like a child. Elizabeth shyly rested her hand on his arm and turned her blushing face to the side.

It was a magnificent view, one that the empress loved and was proud of. All the way to the lighthouse, Elizabeth was distracted by the sweet smell of flowers mixed with the salty air. Her white dress was fluttering under the fierce wind, a remnant of the storm, making it cling to her delicate silhouette.

Leonhardt was worried that she might be cold, so he placed his jacket on Elizabeth's shoulders. His distinctive mint scent, the clear smell of the sea after all the bad things had receded, and the scent of wildflowers seemed to spread through Elizabeth's body to the tips of her fingers every time she took a breath.

Chairs had been prepared behind the lighthouse, waiting for the imperial family. Noticing fences in front of the chairs, Leonhardt finally let go of the breath he had been holding. There were fences, there was his father, and there was Elizabeth—who had somehow taken a seat next to his mother. It felt like what he was worried about wouldn't happen.

Still, Leonhardt kept on looking at the empress' side profile... just in case. As the golden sun began to set, he admired the beauty of the side of her face, the golden line of the sun's light descending over her.

Was mother always this beautiful? For a moment, Leonhardt forgot to breathe as he watched the empress.

"Beautiful, isn't it?"

"It is beautiful. It is as if mother is covered by a thin veil dyed with golden and orange."

"You rascal, it's my job to look at the empress. You just look at your fiancée."

"Is that what you meant? If it's Elizabeth, I need not necessarily..." *Mention it.* Leonhardt couldn't even finish his sentence before he gaped. Seeing that, the emperor smirked. The setting sun was a very good thing for the two men.

The empress and Elizabeth etched in their minds the sight of the sunset, as gorgeous as fireworks and shining as gold, reflected on the sea like a mirror smashed into a thousand pieces.

Seeing their other halves like that, the emperor and Leonhardt felt their hearts fluttering. Elizabeth's wonderful silver hair, which gave the Elysiums the name of the Descendants of Angels, was now dyed red as if a valuable ruby oil was poured from the top of her head. As the light shone on her soft cheeks, he could see the delicate down across her skin. She still had a young face, but looking at it now, her high nose bridge, her full lips, and her flushing cheeks had such loveliness and beauty that it wouldn't be an exaggeration to compare her to some goddess. She was still—still not fully bloomed into her graceful womanhood, but she was already a flower that had taken the thickest and largest root in Leonhardt's heart. How beautiful would it be when such a flower was in full bloom?

Leonhardt held back his hand that had unknowingly reached out towards Elizabeth. He gulped. *I can't do this. It should be enough for me to be able to just sit next to her.* Leonhardt cleared his throat as he shoved himself in between the empress and Elizabeth.

The emperor, whom he pushed aside by surprise, took the chance to immediately snatch the empress by her waist strong enough to make her sit on his lap. The two people, who had once been displayed on the front page of the empire's newspaper as the love story of the century, looked into each other's eyes with the burning red sunset in the background. They didn't need any words. A pity they couldn't press their lips together and snuggle into each other a little closer at that moment.

Leonhardt stared at Elizabeth in a daze before turning his head around. Then he yanked Elizabeth from her chair by her hand to move to the side of the lighthouse. *Mother and father, don't they know decency?! I'm going crazy, seriously!* It wasn't like he couldn't understand their feelings, but what exactly were they doing in front of their future daughter-in-law and son?

Elizabeth, who hadn't noticed, just looked at Leonhardt in confusion. "Why here...?"

"Uh, uhh... so... it's because the setting sun from this spot doesn't look too bad either!" Leonhardt took a seat on top of the grass. He could see the empress' skirt from the corner of his eyes.

The setting sun and the night sky before them swirled like paint on a canvas, unfurling into one spectacular view after another. Leonhardt spread his jacket out for Elizabeth to sit on. When was the last time they had been left alone like this? It felt like it was recent, yet so long at the same time.

Leonhardt glanced to check on Elizabeth before scooting his butt closer to her. He gathered his courage a little more before sneakily shifting his hand towards Elizabeth's hand, which was placed on the ground, while pretending to be clueless.

"Geez, Leonhardt is a fool!" Elizabeth had already noticed him since the time he shifted his butt around and was just waiting to see what he would do. In the end, she let out a sigh and linked her hand with Leonhardt's first. Elizabeth secretly wished that she could pretend to be innocent and just kiss him, like the protagonists in the novels.

If she did that, she felt like her peacefully beating heart would explode.

However, what Leonhardt managed to say, his face flushing red was, "I-it's because you're prettier than the setting sun."

It was just the same silly comment. Elizabeth's shoulders rose and fell as she let out a sigh. She tapped her cheek, inviting him. She didn't know where she got the courage, but her body was moving on its own.

Leonhardt was conflicted for a while. Elizabeth closed her eyes, tapping her rosy cheek with a trembling finger.

What does she want me to do? Is it what I'm thinking of? Is it? Screw it. Leonhardt closed his eyes and used all of his strength to lean forward and press his lips against Elizabeth's soft cheek. His senses went dizzy for a moment with the charming scent and softness, like a rose that bloomed in secret before the dew had even cleared.

Is it okay to have my heart beat this hard? Leonhardt backed off, suddenly terrified.

Elizabeth then slowly opened her eyes. She grabbed some grass, pulled it, and chucked it at Leonhardt. "Crown Prince Leonhardt is such a fool!"

Contrary to her words, her little heart simmered and burned from that single kiss on the cheek.

FIFTY-TWO

Unlike the engineers, who were worried that the stage might collapse due to the heavy rain and wind, the actors, who had to memorize a new script in a hurry, felt relieved when the performance was postponed.

With the storm gone, the leading actress—this generation's best soprano, Miuccia Euterpe—peeked through the curtain to estimate how many people were coming. People were filling the seats and even the passages in between because they expected to see not only the drama festival but also the imperial family.

"Are you nervous?" Avon asked as he tapped on Miuccia's back.

Miuccia shook her head and smiled confidently, her eyes sparkling like black pearls. The best stage and the best audience were waiting for them. Miuccia was certain that tonight was going to be the best night of everyone's lives.

"This is my first time having this kind of performance."

According to the rules, the emperor's seat should be in the middle, where no one could approach it. For example, on an outdoor stage like this where everyone was swarming around, the Imperial Order of Knights and other guards would normally possess the seats all around the emperor. However, the emperor had reduced the number of his guards to allow the public to take the seats instead.

"Everyone here serves as my guard, anyway. What is there to worry about?" With that, the emperor dismissed any opposition and took his seat.

It wasn't like Elizabeth had never been to an opera or a recital with Leonhardt before, but they had always been seated at a special boxed seat for the imperial family. Sitting so close to other people like this felt new and exciting for her.

"Lizzie, come sit a little closer. Do you feel uncomfortable?"

"I'm so giddy! Not at all!"

"That's a relief, but..."

As the final preparations were made for the curtain to be lifted, everyone behind it took a peek at the imperial family. The one who showed his dignity as the emperor and his faith in the people by keeping the amount of guards to a minimum, His Majesty the Emperor. The one who was sitting elegantly next to him with her face gentle yet full of expectation, Her Majesty the Empress. Then the one who inherited only the exceptional parts from those two, the one extolled as a young sword master as well as the future emperor, the Crown Prince. And finally, his beautiful fiancée, who had not officially been announced as the Crown Princess yet but had grown up with the Crown Prince since she was young, and the one who was rumored to have wandered around the market street during the festival.

They naturally inspired people, making them look on with awe or bowed heads. Rather than making a long and exhausting speech, the emperor just greeted them by telling them to enjoy the moment.

The curtain rose.

With a magnificent orchestra recital and the motion done by the latest stage equipment, the stage that previously had nothing turned into a kingdom of mermaids beneath the sea.

Once the curtain fell and rose again, the scene also changed. The lighting that was blue earlier had changed to yellow, and there was a huge sailing ship riding the waves instead of a castle made of coral.

The lighting focused on the prince atop the ship and the naive Little Mermaid who gazed at the prince, on the other side of the stage. The crashing waves drowned out any other sound, and the audience was silent. In the middle of such a stage, the two people's lines alternated and overlapped with each other before separating again.

Elizabeth clasped her hands together as she kept her eyes on the female lead playing the Little Mermaid. The fancy stage makeup didn't look too much at all. Rather, it looked rather naturally fitting for the beautiful lady, who showed different expressions in each scene. The expression of the most innocent princess of the sea when she looked at a spoon, thinking it was a mirror.

The look of surprise, bordering on shock, crossed her face when her eyes locked with the prince's. And when she faced the audience, as she sang a song with the prince, her eyes were full of deep love for him.

How can someone change their expressions like that? Elizabeth nervously watched the scene where the Little Mermaid went to find the witch.

Unlike the villainous role of the witch that people were used to, the witch in this play was completely helpful to the Little Mermaid. She raised the waves so the Little Mermaid could meet the prince again, gave her the human legs she wanted, and even gave her the necessary knowledge she needed to live among the humans. However, in exchange, she just asked for the Little Mermaid's voice and a drop of her blood that contained her beauty.

Elizabeth knew better than anyone that all magic must have a price, but because of how good the actors' acting was, she found herself feeling flabbergasted at the witch just like everybody else.

After getting her legs, being given a ride by the witch on a large seahorse carriage, and going up the seashore, the Little Mermaid suffered in the air up on land that was so different from under the water. She lost consciousness.

And so, the curtain dropped, and the First Act ended.

"What do you think?" Leonhardt asked Elizabeth, who had been gasping since the scene where the Little Mermaid came out on land, grabbed onto her neck, and choked on the air.

It took some time for Elizabeth to barely be able to calm down. She asked Leonhardt, excited, "That actress, can we perhaps meet her after the performance?"

Hearing that, Leonhardt looked up behind him. The emperor nodded. The empress called for a servant to order a bouquet of flowers along with a message card.

"It would not be too bad to give an unforgettable present to the actors who had given us an unforgettable time. Your Majesty, how about calling them over to the palace?"

"That is a good idea. Come to think of it, I heard that a lot of nobles wanted to watch the drama festival but ended up unable to do so due to having to watch with the commoners. Those fools... let us give them a wonderful chance."

The curtain rose again. How would that actress act now that she had lost her voice and had to communicate with her co-stars through gestures and expressions only? Elizabeth once again held her hands together to lift the opera glasses up, focusing on each of the actress' hand gestures and expressions.

There were so many ways to express like and love without having to say it out loud. The action of lifting her hand as if she was clutching her heart, smiling as she rained flower petals on the head of the person she loved, approaching him in secret and hugging him, and others. Although it looked just like the fun and games between a countryside maiden and a naive young man to match, Elizabeth and all the audience had become so immersed in the couple's affection.

However, the pair's happiness didn't last long. The nobles began to persuade the queen, arguing that a person of unknown upbringing and identity, who couldn't even speak, couldn't possibly marry the prince. They tossed out sarcastic comments and malicious remarks about how it couldn't be helped since she was of low birth, even though it was natural that she wouldn't know the nobles' etiquette since she was encountering it for the first time.

Leonhardt clenched his fists.

She couldn't talk, but her ears were wide open. The Little Mermaid desperately studied to be a suitable lady for the imperial court. She learned the humans' alphabets, their etiquette, stopped dancing freely and began to waltz instead. Whenever she danced, the Little Mermaid would lift her skirt and show her soft white legs that had never stepped on the ground. Seeing her feet slowly get dyed in fake blood, Elizabeth was reminded of her own past.

Once, in her childhood that she couldn't even remember now, had she ever danced that flawlessly?

The Little Mermaid who could make everyone smile was no longer there. What replaced her was an empty shell of someone who had drained all of herself and filled it with something else to be the Crown Princess. The eyes that had looked so clear and sparkling disappeared in an instant. Even so, the Little Mermaid endured all that pain because of one person: the prince.

With a violin playing a quiet, mournful sound, the actress laid out her pain, loneliness, and conflict through her body gestures. As she spread her arms and legs, spinning around like a whirlwind as if her body were about to explode, she suddenly hugged herself and dropped—as if she were afraid. Even so, in another scene, when she gazed up at the sky, needing to keep trying, determined not to give up, she seemed another person.

While the Little Mermaid exchanged her freedom for love, slowly withering, the prince was getting pushed out of the competition for the throne.

Will you give up on the throne because you're blinded by your love with such a lowly woman? Or will you rise up to claim the throne by making a princess from another nation your queen, just as has been decided beforehand?

The prince was torn.

As he watched the scene where the prince faced his true self in front of the mirror, Leonhardt was reminded of himself when he had gone to meet Mimir, the master of the Clock Tower. He rooted for the prince in his heart. He didn't need to worry since he was the one who had changed the ending. But he wanted to whisper to the prince that he shouldn't miss his chance so he wouldn't regret anything later.

The witch came up to the land in secret to check how the Little Mermaid was doing, but when she found the beautiful, lively princess she had coveted had been replaced by an elegant lady with empty eyes in the cave by the beach, she sighed.

The witch told her that she could give her mermaid tails back if she wished. She could give her voice back as well, but in exchange, she warned that the Little Mermaid might not be able to stay by the prince's side as a result.

The princess held up a clock, signifying her need for more time to think. Meanwhile, the prince was watching all of their conversation and gestures while hidden behind the shadows of the cave.

Finally, the long-awaited climax and ending scenes played out. The Little Mermaid danced like crazy to find what it was that she really wanted and chased out all the inner conflicts from her body.

The Little Mermaid's maid had made her decision.

At the same time, the prince had to decide.

The Little Mermaid who needed freedom, and the prince loved her so much he couldn't bear to stop her. He abandoned his crown on the bed and ran to the Little Mermaid.

"My love, let us go back to the sea together. You need the sea to live, and I need you. I would rather throw away everything and become a sailor to be able to roam the sea with you."

The Little Mermaid lifted her hands in surprise and disbelief, but the prince looked very serious.

Sick of the battle for the throne, the prince smiled at her, blushing. He scratched the back of his head sheepishly and admitted that he had wanted to be a sailor since the moment he first saw her. "If I became a sailor... would I not be able to meet you once more one day during my voyage? That was what I thought."

The Little Mermaid kept opening her mouth as if she wanted to say something, but her voice was so broken that she couldn't even form a single word. It sounded so hideous that one might doubt she was the same person who had the most beautiful singing voice among her sisters in the sea in the First Act.

The actress teared up. The Little Mermaid pulled the prince into a hug. The curtain fell and rose again.

The Little Mermaid was singing her love story in her beautiful voice. Her lower half, with rainbow scales, was proof that she chose freedom in the end. As she looked at her face reflected on the spoon she held, the Little Mermaid burst into a cheerful laugh—as if she had never lost her light in the first place.

A large ship approached the rock she sat on. The one who appeared leaning over the banister was not the fleet commander, nor was it the chief officer. It was the prince, who was the lowest ranked sailor.

The Little Mermaid waved her hand at the prince and sang a song to calm the waves and call the fair wind. The prince, who had received the captain's permission to go down to the sea where the Little Mermaid was, brushed his hand through her hair.

The Little Mermaid quietly smiled as she threw herself in his embrace and kissed him. Even if the witch pretended to grumble that her plan had gone awry, away from the others, she mumbled that this kind of ending was not so bad either.

With the two people singing a song for each other together until the end, the curtain finally fell. The first to give a standing ovation was the emperor, and the empress was wiping her tears with her third handkerchief.

Who would dare to grumble when the emperor had begun to give his applause? The people stood up from their seats and offered thunderous applause and cheers for the actors, who came back up on stage for the curtain call.

"Your Majesty." The emperor carefully listened to the empress, who couldn't separate the handkerchief from her face, and looked after her in worry.

"If Your Majesty had also had the option to give up on the throne, would I have been happier?"

Both the emperor and Leonhardt, who was sitting in front of them, froze at her words.

"Please never mind. It was mere jest. I am already looking forward to the day when they come to the imperial palace."

Leonhardt gave his handkerchief to Elizabeth, who had started sniffling. Just as she requested earlier, they headed backstage, accompanied by only one guard. The bouquet that the empress ordered had already arrived, so the two brainstormed what they should write on the card. Finally, they knocked on the leading actress' dressing room door, bouquet in hand.

CHAPTER
FIFTY-THREE

After hearing that little guests from the imperial court had come to visit her, Miuccia welcomed them with open arms. "I shall treasure this flower," Miuccia smiled all the way up to her crescent eyes when she accepted the bouquet from Leonhardt.

Elizabeth had completely fallen for Miuccia. To Elizabeth, Miuccia's acting seemed like the very spirit of the character had entered her body. She said, "Umm, Miss Miuccia..."

"Please feel free to call me Miu, Your Future Majesty."

Elizabeth's cheeks flushed red. "H-how do you act like that? You were like..."

"Like a different person?"

Elizabeth nodded fervently.

Miuccia gave a smile as gorgeous as a summer rose. She bent down to meet Elizabeth's eyes. "I empty myself and fill back up. I lift my emotions to new extremes and fool myself into thinking that I am the protagonist and the one who drives the story."

"Fool... yourself...?"

Miuccia picked a small rose bud mixed in the bouquet and passed it over to Elizabeth. "If I want to fool myself, I have to be honest with myself. If I know what my real feelings are, the rest becomes fairly easy."

She couldn't relate to what she was saying at all, but Elizabeth held dear the flower that her yearned actress gave her. "Be honest... with myself..." *What feelings am I feeling right now? Yearning? Joy? Delight?*

"That is correct! What kind of feelings appear when you look right next at His Highness the Crown Prince?" Miuccia smiled mischievously as she studied Elizabeth and Leonhardt.

Leonhardt flinched, surprised.

"When I look at Leon...?" Elizabeth's clear blue eyes fixed on him.

Leon shifted, awkwardly scratching the back of his head.

"Do you get angry? Or do you feel happy? Sad? Bliss? Does your heart flutter? What kind of fluttering is it? Do you think you want to possess him? Do you want to stay by his side?"

"Miuccia."

"Does Your Highness feel the same?"

Leonhardt froze in his place, just like someone whose embarrassing secrets had been exposed. On the other hand, Elizabeth was hiding her expression behind the small flower.

"My goodness! So, it is love."

"Love, you say. We're still..."

"Feeling affection for each other, cherishing each other, not wanting to be separated even for a moment, wanting to do every single thing together, being greedy for that person yet also fearing that your greed might hurt them, showing your ugly side to them and regretting it afterwards, yearning for them once night comes, and feeling your heart flutter when you see them. If that is not love, then what is?" Miuccia sang in a single breath, like only a star could. She told Elizabeth and Leonhardt, "The two of you suit each other so well."

"H-how are you so sure of that?"

"Oh my, does that mean Your Highness does not wish to be so?"

"That is not it...!"

Miuccia stared at him with suspicion before smiling and lowering her gaze again along with the sound of the wave's foam breaking. "It was truly an honor to have you personally come and let me have this encounter. Your Highness, Lady Elizabeth."

"Oh, um. Sure. It was an exceptional performance. It would be wonderful if we could meet again in the imperial palace soon."

"Will the stage be awaiting us?" Miuccia's black eyes sparkled like the stars reflected in the sea.

"I have no confidence that we can be the audience that satisfies you, but will you come if the stage awaits you?" Leonhardt said.

Miuccia chuckled. "If the stage awaits us, then we certainly must go! I shall look forward to that day. The day has gone dark, so please be careful on your way back."

Miuccia escorted Leonhardt and Elizabeth outside where the imperial carriage was already waiting. Miuccia curtsied to the emperor and the empress.

The emperor responded, "We shall see you in the imperial palace soon. We will have to get started now if we want to build a stage suitable for you."

"It would be my honor, Your Majesty. I hope that my skills were able to serve as a diversion for Her Majesty the Empress."

"I feel a lot better thanks to Miuccia's songs. If another prenatal care is required at the palace, we will have to call you over then."

"Oh dear, I look forward to seeing which would be faster between my throat resting and the imperial family members increasing!"

The empress laughed at Miuccia's words.

"Umm, father, mother."

"What is it, Crown Prince?"

"We would like to go back by foot. Will that be fine?"

Elizabeth was looking at Miuccia, who still seemed to glitter with confidence even in front of the emperor and the empress. When Leonhardt asked to walk, Elizabeth turned, feeling as if a bucket of ice water had been poured on her head.

The emperor and the empress also looked equally shocked.

"Tomorrow's onboard party will be our last event, won't it? I would like to show Lizzie the ordinary city streets at night."

Miuccia smirked and pretended to be innocent as she spilled some information that Elizabeth might get excited for. "Passing through the maze-like canals surrounding the city on a small ferry is quite tasteful, especially on a night when it's hard to tell where the sky ends and the sea begins."

Both Elizabeth and Leonhardt immediately looked up at the emperor and the empress with pleading eyes. Miuccia just coyly batted her eyelashes. The emperor and the empress gave a hearty laugh as they gave their permission, telling the teens not to come home too late.

The city that had the most beautiful sea in the empire was also known for having canals around each alley, just like a maze. After the ferryman offered to take them on a light trip around the city canals for an hour, Leonhardt and Elizabeth boarded the ferry.

"Kyaaah!"

In case Elizabeth might trip in the dark under a mere soft light, Leonhardt swooped her up and carried her down to the ferry.

As the ferryman began to paddle the long oar and steer the ferry with much skill, Leonhardt sat by Elizabeth's side and gently placed his hand on top of hers.

"We should've come here during the day as well if we'd known this exists."

"Let's come again next year."

"I feel like the things we'll have to do will increase by next year...?"

Elizabeth and Leonhardt looked at each other and chuckled. The ferryman started to sing a song about the city's patron saint in a low voice for the young lovers.

"Take us there for a moment," Leonhardt said as he pointed at a shipboard market that was about to close for the day.

From a market boat filled with flowers, Leonhardt picked lilies of the valley and blue forget-me-nots that resembled Elizabeth. He also bought flowers that were turning more fragrant as the night went on. He wove them into a flower crown with deft fingers. "What do you think?"

Elizabeth cast her gaze downwards and lowered her head.

He placed the scent of summer woven into a flower crown on her head, to which Elizabeth responded with a smile that Leonhardt valued above anything else.

The single hour was too short for the couple to exchange more than a few words. When Elizabeth and Leonhardt saw a lamp in the canal to write wishes on, they made the same one.

Please let us come here again next year and have a beautiful time together.

Leonhardt had given the ferryman plenty of tips for giving Elizabeth an unforgettable experience.

The Crown Prince stepped off the ferry first and extended his hand to Elizabeth.

Elizabeth carefully rose from her seat and placed her hand on Leonhardt's. It was the same hand that had been on top of hers earlier, but now her fingers that touched his felt hot. After gathering some courage, Elizabeth jumped out of the ferry. Leonhardt caught her with ease. In each other's arms, both Elizabeth and Leonhardt blushed up to their ears.

On the way back to the mansion, the market was closing, and the night wind blew coldly. The pair felt nervous as they walked, afraid that the other would hear the sound of their heart.

"You two kids over there, would you like your fortune to be told?"

In reflex, Leonhardt twisted his body towards the voice and readied his hand on the sword at his waist. Elizabeth, who was prepared to throw rocks from behind him if necessary, noticed a hand, dry like an old tree, beckoning them from an alleyway.

"No need to be so alert. What can an old fortuneteller even curse you youngsters with?"

"Who are you?" Leonhardt headed toward the alley, still on full alert.

In the narrow corridor, an old woman in an older robe was sitting across at a table, looking as suspicious as she possibly could. On the table stained with fingermarks, there was a wad of faded, worn cards and a large glass sphere.

"I'll make it free since I get to meet such honorable people," cooed the crone. "Aren't you curious about your romantic fortune?"

"Romantic fortune?!"

"Oh dear, I feel like I just heard a lion that hasn't completely matured its roar. I guess I'm getting old."

"Lizzie, let's ignore her. There's no need to deal with her." Leonhardt hinted at his displeasure as he pulled on Elizabeth.

However, since arriving, Elizabeth had been immersed in the atmosphere, one like she had never experienced in the imperial palace. As if she couldn't hear what Leonhardt was saying, Elizabeth pushed him aside and approached the fortuneteller.

"Young miss, you look like you have a lot of things you're curious about. I can tell you everything, or I can tell you just one thing."

"Can you... really find out?"

"What do you want to find out?" The fortuneteller, her face hidden behind her hood, grinned. Her teeth, which had gone yellow, glistened like a beast's.

"Lizzie, we should just go."

"But aren't you curious, Leon? We can find out about our future."

There is no one in this world who knows better than me about what's going to happen in the future, so let's just go! Leonhardt sighed in frustration and just kicked a pebble on the ground.

"Okay." Elizabeth followed Leonhardt, looking downcast.

Leonhardt glanced behind briefly before looking up at the sky and became conflicted. He sighed. "Mimir from the Clock Tower would've been much more reliable."

When Elizabeth realized what he meant, she grinned and ran back to the fortune teller.

If she says she wants something with that face... I end up wanting to give her anything, even if it's the most valuable thing in the world... Leonhardt sighed again and glared at the fortuneteller, as if telling her that she better not lie if they were going to listen to her.

"Don't make such a scary face. All right, let's see... a noble young master and his fiancée, is it? Let's see from the lady first..."

With a nimble flick of her wrinkled wrist, the fortuneteller mixed the cards and spread them in a semicircle shape. "The lady must pick one first, and the young master then picks one. After that, both of you must pick one card together."

Elizabeth picked her card, her heart fluttering. Even though Leonhardt acted like he really didn't want to, he thought hard about which card to pick when his turn came. For the final card, Leonhardt let Elizabeth pick an option first. Elizabeth shook her head and put her hand under the table as she told Leonhardt to pick a card again. The fortuneteller just rested her chin in her hand and smiled as she watched the two of them.

After some debate—both of them wanted to let the other choose—they finally agreed to choose the card in the very center. Elizabeth placed her fair hand on top of Leonhardt's.

"Okay, let's see... how deep your bond is... Huh?"

The fortune teller rose from her seat halfway and kept muttering in a daze—as if she just saw something unbelievable. Both became wary of the fortuneteller again; Elizabeth with curiosity and Leonhardt with doubt.

"So, what do the cards say?" Leonhardt snarled, as if he would rip apart the cards—or whatever else—if needed. Elizabeth stayed by his side, nodding repeatedly.

After clearing her throat and stretching her body for a moment, the fortuneteller finally turned over the cards picked by Elizabeth, Leonhardt, and the two of them together.

"This is..."

"No way..."

Leonhardt and Elizabeth over the table so far it looked like they would fall on their faces. There was nothing on the three cards. Only faded colors.

"What is this scam?"

"What do you mean scam?! Who would dare to scam you? Neither of you seem to have any aptitude for magic. These cards can only be seen through mana."

"That's what a scammer would say."

"Young lady, can't you shut that young master up?"

Caught up in her interest in the strange atmosphere, Elizabeth held tightly onto Leonhardt's hem.

The fortuneteller explained, "First of all, our young lady right here... seems to still be unable to figure out her feelings. This is a mountain. It's a tall and steep mountain that you have to overcome by yourself without other people's help. Once you pass that mountain, a heaven on earth where you can find a flower made of gold and a stream of silver on a ground made of silk awaits you!"

"Moun...tain? My feelings?" Elizabeth murmured in a daze.

The fortuneteller, however, did not elaborate further and moved on to Leonhardt's card. "Our young master, on the other hand... Hoho, you should've acted better before you regretted that much."

Leonhardt frowned at that comment and rested his hand on his sword handle again.

"Though, it seems like you're working hard, all right. However, you must not forget: the consequences of past mistakes will inevitably return in some form or another."

"If you're going to say ominous things, it would be better to not say anything at all." If he could, he would've dragged her out of this alley and handed her over to the neighborhood watch already.

The fortuneteller grinned and explained the last card, "And so the prince prepared a flowery path and the most beautiful landscape in the world for the princess. But whether she will walk on it or not lies with the princess. young lady, young master. Be cautious when you make your decisions. Then everything will go well."

"What kind of interpretation is that?" Leonhardt mumbled, sounding exasperated.

Elizabeth just tilted her head.

"Forget it, we're just wasting our time here. Let's go back before it's late. It would be better for us to call for a carriage." Leonhardt stood up from his seat. Fortunately, he was able to easily call for a carriage from the nearest inn. Leonhardt let Elizabeth get on the carriage first, glaring back at the fortuneteller in the alley.

"No need to make such a scary face. Having said that, you must never forget. Now that you've gone as far as turning back time, what do you need to do from now on to make her happy?"

"What does that..."

The fortuneteller raised her finger and made a shushing gesture. The finger that looked like a drying old tree had disappeared and, in its place, fiery red hair and thin arms as white as a statue were revealed at the edges of her robe.

Leonhardt doubted his eyes.

However, the carriage had set off. When Leonhardt turned back for a moment, only the wind was blowing in the alley—as if there had been nothing there from the start.

"…Lizzie."

"Yes?"

Inside the carriage taking them back to the mansion, Leonhardt called out Elizabeth's name as he stared out of the window. "Elizabeth, can't you stop time and just stay by my side always?"

A bunch of question marks seemed to pop up on Elizabeth's face.

Leonhardt then said it was nothing, shaking his head and leaning his face on the cold glass window.

"I'll always be by Leon's side though? No matter how quickly time passes or how quickly or slowly I grow. Leon, are you perhaps worried that I'll be bigger than you?"

Along with the fluttering sound of fabric, a warm scent softer than anything in the world spread out over Leonhardt's shoulder.

"Ugh, that's right. I'm so worried that you'll be as big as Sir Bern, that's why I told you to slow time." Leonhardt grinned and loosely wrapped Elizabeth's silver hair around his finger.

By the time they arrived at the mansion, Elizabeth had become absolutely exhausted and hungry. Leonhardt refused the servants who offered to help; he carried her up the stairs himself. The weight on his back felt lighter than his favorite sword.

What if she flies away like a feather? Leonhardt kept glancing at his back to check whether Elizabeth was asleep. He left the task of changing her clothes to the maids.

Once the maids took their leave, Leonhardt peeked from behind the partition and placed a light kiss on Elizabeth's cheek. She was sleeping soundly, covered by a summer blanket.

Elizabeth grumbled in her sleep, maybe because his breath brushed against the fine hair on her cheek. She turned to her side.

Leonhardt, who was frozen in a bent-over state, realized what a shameless thing he had just done. He took several steps backward. *Are you crazy? Even if your bodies are the same age, your mind has seen more years. Knock it off!*

Since he first met her, it was as if the rationality of adulthood that had been restraining him had begun to urge him to leap over the terrace and into the sea.

With his face flushed red, Leonhardt just took a forget-me-not flower from the wreath beside Elizabeth's pillow before rushing out of the room.

To avoid the chaotic atmosphere of packing up to go back to the imperial palace, the pair decided to spend the rest of their time at the beach, in the city, or any other place before the onboard party started. This time, they were going out officially accompanied by the guards.

Elizabeth and Leonhardt each carried a cold drink as they roamed the high-class shopping district. Whenever Elizabeth found something interesting in a glass display, Leonhardt suggested he buy it for her. Elizabeth then shook her head, saying she was already so happy just looking at it, so much that it felt as though she were walking on a cloud.

After wandering around the shopping district the entire afternoon, the two of them took a seat on the edge of the fountain and began to discuss what they should buy as a souvenir.

"How about a knitted light shawl? Apparently, the knitting here is mixed with the method of mending the fishermen's nets, so it gives a completely original feel."

"Or a sculpture made from corals? We'll make one that looks like you, Lizzie, with white corals and pearls for the pedestal..."

"His Majesty the Emperor would suit something like that."

"I'm talking about you though..." Leonhardt awkwardly scratched his cheek.

"How about we find something memorable to us and borrow Her Majesty's treasure vault and put it there?" Elizabeth said after a moment of thinking with her hand under her chin. Leonhardt agreed, saying it was a good idea.

"A clamshell necklace?"

"That would be best, wouldn't it?" Leonhardt rose from his seat and extended his hand to Elizabeth. Elizabeth had been sitting on Leonhardt's handkerchief earlier, so she lightly dusted the handkerchief in the air before folding it neatly and returning it. The couple, along with their guards, walked one more lap around the shopping district to find a souvenir.

Corals and pearls, a mother-of-pearl decoration that shone a rainbow, and so on. All of them looked suitable to commemorate the summer, so it was difficult to pick one.

"It is time to make our leave, Your Highness."

"Already?" Leonhardt and Elizabeth raised their voices at the same time. They had just been about to find an item they liked, but it was time for them to go prepare for the party.

"Let's definitely come back next year."

"Let's prepare a list of things to do before we come next time."

The pair trudged onward, holding each other's hands.

All the nobles from the surrounding territories, local officials, and the ones who played a great role in the drama festival had come aboard the large ship prepared for the party. The wooden floor sparkled after the sailors, who had given Elizabeth spiked water, wiped it with tears of repentance, with regret as the oil.

All kinds of fresh seafood dishes were presented along with a red—not white—wine, and soon the empress and the emperor appeared hand in hand as the party's stars. The emperor made a light speech comparing the empire, the imperial family, the nobles, and the people to a sailing ship as he tapped on the key in front of him. Beside him, the empress smiled serenely.

Before long, the emperor and the empress walked down into the crowd, the rounds of applause serving as their red carpet. Not knowing when he would see the empress again, the mansion's chef presented fresh oysters with lemon for her. The people sensitive to the fishy smell of raw seafood took half a step back. The empress beamed, touching her hand to her chest, and invited the chef to come to the imperial palace. Although the chef refused her offer, saying that the kitchen needed someone to lead it, his face already showed the dignity of an imperial chef.

But the moment the empress slid the oyster into her mouth, the chef's expression turned blue.

"Ugh...!" The chef wasn't the only one whose face was turning blue.

Held up by maids from either side, the empress threw up everything over the ship's banister. The emperor's and Leonhardt's faces both turned as white as a sheet. Suddenly, the chef found himself helplessly surrounded by guards, trembling.

Leonhardt grabbed an oyster and sniffed it. "Is it poison?"

There was a possibility of the poison's unique smell being covered by the seafood's fishy scent, but after making the chef eat a few of the other oysters just in case, it was discovered that there was nothing wrong with the oysters. That meant that the empress was nauseous for another reason. The doctor, who was told to stand by at all times because the empress had been sick recently, came into the cabin in a hurry to attend to the empress.

The chef, who had almost been falsely charged with poisoning the empress; Leonhardt, who would do almost anything to prevent the future where the empress died; the emperor, who wished to protect his beloved wife; and all the imperial court members who didn't want to lose Her Majesty the Empress who treated them even more kindly than their own mothers—all waited anxiously for the doctor to return.

Eventually, the doctor exited the ship's cabin. For some reason, he couldn't suppress his smile. The emperor darted over and grabbed him by his collar, lifting him up into the air.

As Leonhardt and the guard tried to stop the emperor, the doctor coughed as he said his congratulations with much difficulty, "Congratulations, Your... Ugh... Your Majesty! Her Majesty... Ack... Her Majesty... Phew..." The doctor fixed his collar after Leonhardt helped him set his foot back on the deck. "Thank you, Your Highness. Ahem, ahem... Her Majesty has conceived!"

The crowd's expressions began to shift. Someone was sincerely congratulating the empress' pregnancy, another one was predicting that the political spectrum and the successor of the throne might change, another one was just feeling relieved that she was safe. As for Leonhardt, he wasn't sure how to react upon hearing that he was going to have a younger sibling despite having lived as an only child all his life.

This... This never happened before. A younger sibling. No way. I... I... Damn it!

"Leon, what's wrong? Did you perhaps drink alcohol?"

"I'm just surprised mother has suddenly conceived. I'm fine. Can you congratulate her for me? I need to get some air." Leonhardt still showed Elizabeth a smile so she wouldn't worry, even if he was getting an awful headache.

Elizabeth still looked doubtful even as she entered the cabin with the emperor.

The onboard party was changed into a party to celebrate the empress' pregnancy. The band delightfully performed lively music, and everyone drank and danced after hearing such joyful news.

Only Leonhardt was suffering, hidden away as he clutched his head, feeling like it might crack open due to the pain of his memories being erased.

THE CLOCK TOWER'S TEA TIME

CHAPTER
FIFTY-FIVE

The wind no longer carried the scent of the sea. Instead, it brought the ripe fruits and petals of summer blossoms. After returning to the imperial palace, the imperial family resumed their daily routine. While the emperor was busy taking care of all the state affairs that had become overdue, he had also been looking out for the empress' condition every day that he felt like even splitting himself into three wouldn't be enough.

"One body would be to work on the state affairs, another one would be throwing the imperial law books at the heads of those who are trying to do something ridiculous, and the last one I'd like it to be dedicated entirely for my love."

The empress' morning sickness was so severe that she was struggling to even drink water for a while. Instead of showing the typical signs of pregnancy, she grew thinner. The emperor grabbed the innocent doctors by the collar and shook them. When in the middle of the night the empress mumbled in her sleep that she was hungry, the emperor personally rushed down to the imperial kitchen.

When the maids saw Elizabeth coming back after some time apart with not just a bigger body, but a bigger heart as well, they teared up behind her back. The doll-like young lady who had trembled when she first arrived now laughed and wandered around like a free bird. She had also become much better at expressing her feelings. The moment she saw Bailey, Elizabeth grinned so broadly and expressed such love that she couldn't be called a doll anymore. Above all, the maids didn't know what had happened at the seaside, but they felt a fresh new joy, like a bright green apple, whenever they saw Elizabeth and Leonhardt together.

"It must be that, right? It must be," the maids whispered to each other as they watched Leonhardt and Elizabeth, who were having a cold spell of spring by themselves when everyone else was heading towards midsummer.

While everyone else resumed their positions, Leonhardt remained seated alone, scowling. The first thing he had done when he returned to the imperial palace was to check the cipher when everyone else was asleep, save for the minimum number of personnel.

[■ Month ■ Day: Mother passed away.]

It was definitely written that way in the cipher. However, Mother had not passed away. He was even going to get a younger sibling he had never had before. How was he supposed to take this? First of all, Leonhardt drew an arrow next to the writing "mother passed away" and wrote "little sibling was born."

Come to think of it, something else had changed from the future as well. He had become a sword master. While he felt proud that he managed to awaken as one just because of his feelings of wanting to protect Elizabeth's smile, he was also worried whether he could cultivate this power properly or not.

Leonhardt tucked away the cipher once again and then headed to bed. He felt a bit empty without the sound of waves that he'd started to grow used to.

How did mother manage to endure through this emptiness...?

He tossed this way and turned that way, unable to sleep. After some time, he got up and headed to the spot where the souvenirs from the sea had been put away. Most of them were clam shells, conches, or small coral fragments that kids often kept as treasure, but an especially huge conch caught his eyes. *I took it because I was curious whether it was true that you can hear the sound of waves from inside the conch. Can you really?* Leonhardt carefully lifted the conch and closed his eyes, pressing his ear against it. It felt incomplete since it couldn't perfectly replicate the sound of waves, but the sound of humming tickling his ear was not so bad. Leonhardt took the conch to bed. As he slowly sorted out the things he had to do today, he kept the conch by his ear until he fell asleep.

The next day, Elizabeth headed to the Clock Tower and Leonhardt to the Imperial Order of Knights' building.

"I'll go to the Clock Tower later as well." Leonhardt could now naturally give Elizabeth a kiss on her forehead. He was carrying a well-dried long piece of seaweed. It was troublesome to make up reasons for the maids, who knew the seaweed's value, whenever they asked if it was prepared for his mother. He wanted to use that as an excuse for him to have a bout with Albert, but after seeing Albert get so touched at the gift that he would risk committing treason by switching his allegiance from Leonhardt's father to Leonhardt himself, that feeling cooled down.

"Ahem... ahem... Your Highness, is there something you want to tell me?"

"Not really. Feels like I've said everything I wanted to say and passed the item I needed to pass."

Albert began to groan and fidget.

"Do you want to spar with me?"
Albert grinned and bobbed his head up and down.

"Awakening to protect someone you love... I'm looking forward to seeing how the people will react upon hearing this story."

"Let me know if you found a minstrel with a good mouth. But if you find someone who defiles Lizzie's honor, you may kill them on the spot under my name."

Albert looked proudly at Leonhardt, who had grown so mature these past few months, as they headed to the sparring ground.

After hearing the news that the Crown Prince—who had become a sword master after going to the sea—and the commander of the Imperial Order of Knights were going to spar, the knights started gathering in groups.

Leonhardt steadied his arms to control the aura that jolted around by itself inside him.

"Your Highness, don't restrain it and try to let it flow naturally," Albert advised when he saw Leonhardt grimace.

As much as his aura was created with the pure desire to protect Elizabeth along with anger, it was a ferocious one. It seemed like he needed to calm down to control such an aggressive power. "That's... if it's as easy as you say, would I be like this...?"

Let the aura flow, he says. Easy for him to say. Even though Leonhardt grumbled about it, he still followed Albert's instruction faithfully. The moment he placed the tips of his sword on the ground and let the aura flow, he could feel his arm getting lighter.

"Oh God! Your Highness! I didn't say to turn the sparring ground's floor upside down!"

However, unlike his expectation that his aura would get absorbed into the ground, it tore through the sparring ground's floor, stretched out in hundreds and thousands of branches like a tree branch, and turned it upside down.

"I might really die during our spar at this rate. I know perfectly well how precious my life is, so I think we might have to postpone our spar a little later."

The knights shoveling the wrecked floor of the sparring ground looked at Albert and Leonhardt with a disappointed gaze.

"Let the aura flow. I've thought about it too, but can't you just tell me how?"

"How am I supposed to know? I'm not a sword master. I was just suggesting for Your Highness to try."

"What?"

"That was a joke. Actually, since the moment I heard the news that Your Highness has awakened, I've investigated how the past sword masters trained themselves."

"Did you have any luck learning anything?"

"Throw away all desire to cut through water and mountains and do it like you're cutting a needle vertically and making a hole in the middle of a coin... Lines like that were quite impressive."

Leonhardt groaned as he rested his chin on the table. Albert gave him a glass of cold water as he presented him with a new task. "I'm sure that method was left on record because they were effective. From tomorrow on, Your Highness should participate in the training of chopping off firewood in preparation for winter."

"Firewood... What? Sir Bern, I'm saying this just in case, but it's still summer."

"I know that, too. However, Your Highness, if you continue to use your aura in such a manner, only burnt ashes will remain, not firewood. Perhaps, practicing by cutting firewood could serve as a useful method to hone your control over it? Come winter, I shall pass the word that the firewood was provided that way by Your Highness. Your Highness should also do something befitting a Crown Prince now."

"You certainly have a point... but is it just a feeling or are you dumping a troublesome job on me in the pretext of training?"

"It is just like volunteering for the sake of the people, for the sake of a warm winter for them." Albert personally demonstrated the saying that a smiling face cannot be spit on with his expression. Seeing him like that, Leonhardt shook his head and thought that maybe he shouldn't have brought Albert that seaweed.

After the sparring ground, he headed to the Clock Tower. A little sibling that shouldn't have been born was on its way. This meant that the future had completely changed. What if the baby was a boy, and he was more suitable than Leonhardt to sit on the emperor's throne? Brothers fighting to the point of true violence was just a terrible story people liked to tell, something that happened centuries ago maybe... right?

He should prepare for the worst, like getting dethroned as the Crown Prince.

If that happens, then what about Elizabeth? No, maybe she can live a little more freely if she doesn't become the empress. But if the duke of Elysium resorted to something again...

Leonhardt hastened his steps to the Clock Tower. Thanks to the boatman being contacted in advance, Leonhardt was able to arrive at the Clock Tower in a flash. At the top of the tower, Leonhardt immediately went to find Mimis Brunnr.

"What is this? Even Lizzie brought a souvenir along, but His Highness came empty-handed?" Mimir chattered, eyes as wide and inquisitive as a cat's.

They were about to start their teatime. On the table between Mimir and Elizabeth was a box filled with chocolates shaped like shells and seahorses.

"Should I spare a room for Your Highness?" Mimir asked out of courtesy. However, Leonhardt shook his head and headed to Mimis Brunnr's research room.

"Do you want me to set aside Leon's portion?"

"I would be thankful for that. Flip the table upside down if Mimir gives you something weird to eat, Lizzie."

"You think I'm crazy? Why would I do that to Lizzie, who's not like you, Your Highness?"

"Big Sis Mimir! That's an attempted assassination against the imperial family..."

Leonhardt chuckled as he opened the door to Mimis Brunnr's research room. The room where the master of the Clock Tower dwelled was as messy as always. The ceiling and the ground were flipped upside down, making it difficult for Leonhardt to move around. He closed his eyes for a moment, starting to feel dizzy.

"What brings you here today?" Mimis Brunnr asked, basking in the sunlight coming in from the windows on the roof, as he relaxed with a book on the ceiling—or more like the floor attached to the ceiling.

Leonhardt bit his lip and pondered for a moment when he realized a chair was suddenly prodding his backside. He sat on it.

"...Mimis Brunnr, supposing that you turned back time from a far future to the past, if a person who was definitely not supposed to be there in the future is still alive and another person that was supposed to be there disappeared... can you still say that it's the same future?"

Mimir Brunnr glanced up with eyes half-buried under long white lashes. He stared at Leonhardt, who had a troubled expression. He asked, "If it is not the same future, does that mean that the future that caused me to go back to the past no longer exists?"

"Can you explain in an easier way?" Leonhardt racked his brain trying to understand Mimis Brunnr's words.

Mimis Brunnr chuckled as he served Leonhardt a cup of tea. Stroking his long beard, he continued, "In other words, it would be like a forked road. If a carriage always follows one path, the other will fade and disappear, eventually even being forgotten by those who used it in the past. This might be a little exaggerated, but, eventually, new landscape will be in its place."

"I can understand it a little now. So that's how it is..."

"Your Highness, be cautious. You have to be cautious in everything. It is more difficult to get a second chance than a first chance."

"I will keep that in mind. As always, thank you."

Mimis Brunnr gave a benevolent smile before turning the room—or maybe just Leonhardt's sight—back around.

FIFTY-SIX

Leonhardt was speechless for a moment when he saw the harmonious, affectionate, and happy little scene after coming out of Mimis Brunnr's room.

"Leon!" Elizabeth, who was sitting on a spot right opposite him, waved.

"A crazy cat-like witch, a girl wearing a blue dress, and a boy who resembled a blushing white rabbit? Should I grab a hat somewhere or something?" Leonhardt muttered, moving to take a seat on the chair that Mimir took down from a corner of the ceiling.

As Mimir dropped a cube of sugar into the tea, she introduced the boy, "This is Ilysses Eldirjan von Perian. He's my pupil."

"Ils is your pupil?" Leonhardt almost spurted out his tea.

"G-greetings to the little sun of the empire..." Hearing Leonhardt suddenly call him with a shortened name, Ilysses was so humbled that he panicked.

To protect his dignity as the Crown Prince, Leonhardt chose to gulp down the hot tea instead of spitting it out.

Elizabeth was watching in worry since the tea was so hot that it could burn the roof of his mouth, but Leonhardt tried his hardest to endure the pain and turned his head toward Ilysses.

Although he was shaking like an herbivore in front of a predator, his long-time buddy that had made him realize that—in his life before—he had been an utter idiot, still had the same steady eyes. Leonhardt wanted to hug him and roll on the ground with him if he could. But unfortunately, there was still a long way to go until he could become that friendly with him.

Ilysses felt so much pressure from Leonhardt's gaze, one that seemed almost sentimental. He glanced at the table, at Leonhardt, and then back at the table, fiddling with an empty teacup. *D-did I make some kind of mistake toward His Highness...?*

Not knowing that Ilysses' heart—which had been weak since birth and always worried Leonhardt and the other officials—was racing very hard, Leonhardt stared at him with a daunting look for a while.

Hold on, was Ils also Mimir's pupil in the past? That was not in his memory, but now the future had completely changed. Taking into account Ilysses' inherent desire for knowledge, it wasn't really strange for Mimir to teach him. Leonhardt had mixed feelings when he looked at Ilysses, who had become newly caught up in the completely changed future because of Leonhardt's foolishness.

Come to think of it, there were probably many others whose lives had changed because of him in this timeline. Elizabeth, his mother, and even the younger sibling that hadn't even existed in his old life... For some reason, Leonhardt felt like he had touched on something he shouldn't have.

"What did you talk about with Sir Mimis Brunnr?" Elizabeth changed the topic after seeing that Leonhardt's face had darkened.

"Huh? Oh... I just wanted to say hello to an elder and wish him well..."

"Is that so?" Mimir asked, eyes wide. No matter how he looked at it, she definitely said it as if she couldn't believe that His Highness would do something so mature and polite.

Leonhardt snapped, "Why are you giving me that look?!"

"Goodness me. What did I do...? I just said that because it was unexpected to see Your Highness do something unusual. I sincerely apologize if it offended you."

"Far from sincere, that apology sounds absolutely soulless."

"Oh dear, you got me," Mimir said nonchalantly as she lowered her gaze and emptied her teacup.

Leonhardt glared at Mimir, flabbergasted. Then he shook his head, loosening his shoulders and letting out a sigh.

He heard a small laughter from somewhere. Contrary to Elizabeth, who was already so used to Mimir and Leonhardt bickering that she only smiled, Ilysses was bent over from laughter.

"Ils?"

"Oh! Y-Your Highness! My apologies. That's... so, uh..."

"No need to be so formal. Father called you here because Lizzie and I need a friend. So, wouldn't it be ridiculous to call your friend so stiffly like Your Highness the Crown Prince?"

"But Your Highness..."

"Don't you see how deep in the ground my dignity has fallen just by seeing the way your teacher treats the Crown Prince of her own nation?" Leonhardt made the best pitiful face he could make. Mimir was saying impious things like he was despicable and that Ilysses shouldn't get fooled, but he ignored it. When Ilysses didn't immediately object, Leonhardt swallowed back a sting of sadness.

Although Ilysses had known about him from the behavior of the people in the imperial palace, a little—very little—exaggerated rumor from Mimir, and the stories Lady Elizabeth had told him, the Crown Prince he encountered in reality was more easygoing and even friendlier than he had thought.

Since he still felt timid when facing his teacher, who was four years older than he was, Ilysses was envious of Leonhardt and Elizabeth for being able to treat Mimir so casually. Even if they fought so much it seemed like fate, the relationship between the two seemed like a very candid one.

Also, the fact that all Leonhardt's behavior towards Lady Elizabeth was so sweet was something he had already heard from his father, who attended the welcoming reception in his place because he had been down with a cold. He had thought perhaps it was because they had been promised to each other even before they were born, but they looked at each other with such energy and affection.

"Lizzie, what were you doing? You can't just eat anything this witch gives you. You might get turned into a rabbit at this rate."

"Your Highness doesn't need to worry about that since I've learned a long time ago with your help that I can't recklessly transform someone into something else!"

"Leon, have you turned into a rabbit before...?"

"Ahem, ahem. So, what were you guys talking about again?" *God, that witch, she says anything and everything in front of Lizzie!* Leonhardt grit his teeth as he tilted the kettle. However, instead of the well-brewed tea, there was only the obnoxious rattling sound of ceramics.

"I-I can brew more!"

Leonhardt turned his head to his side again after trying to tilt the kettle a few more times in humiliation.

Ilysses was looking down as he extended his trembling arms forward.

Anyone would think that I'm passing him the national treasure or something... The teacups and kettle they were using actually really were as valuable as national treasures, but Leonhardt just casually placed the kettle on Ilysses' stretched out palm.

While Ilysses went off to brew a new tea, Mimir reclined in her seat, supported her head with her arms, and muttered in an idle manner, "That guy, I don't even have anything else to teach him, but he clings to me every day asking me to teach him magic."

"If it's Ils... does he have no aptitude for magic?"

Mimir, who was swaying her chair back and forth, stopped moving at once and stared at Leonhardt. "How did Your Highness know that?"

Oops. How should he make something up when he couldn't say that he heard it from somewhere or that he heard it from the person himself? Leonhardt's gaze began to waver.

However, Mimir didn't really want to know. She swayed her chair again and continued talking, "This is my first time meeting someone who had so little aptitude for magic after

Lizzie. But since his thirst for knowledge doesn't lose to a Minute Hand, it's sometimes terrifying."

"Do you think that it's a pity?"

Mimir nodded.

"He could have crushed the records of the Clock Tower..."

Leonhardt's eyebrows twitched at Mimir's unexpectedly high opinion of Ilysses. Mimir just kept on staring at the door, where Ilysses left holding the kettle, with a face that seemed to sincerely find it regrettable.

"Oh! Ilysses is super smart." Elizabeth announced, voice bright and high and reminding Leonhardt of lilies.

"Really? What did you talk about with him?" Leonhardt asked as he put a slice of cake on Elizabeth's plate.

"About the waves."

"The waves?"

Elizabeth nodded. "Big Sis Mimir said that it happens because the water spirits jump high and collide with each other, and they scatter into round and white debris, but..."

"But?"

"Something about the moon and gravity. It's still a bit too difficult for Lizzie to know about, so I just rearranged it a little."

"Aren't you just ruining her childhood innocence?" Leonhardt asked.

However, the one whose childhood innocence was ruined, Elizabeth, didn't seem to really care. "Well... that boy is just a plain genius. He can answer you like a dictionary no matter what you ask."

"Also, we were just about to discuss the background of the mermaid's tale, the reason why it was differently presented in each region, and the old culture of the region as seen from the misrepresented tale."

"Mermaid's tale... What?"

Elizabeth had spouted all that without a single breath. For a second, Leonhardt doubted that he heard her properly. For a brief moment, he thought he might be the least intellectual person here.

"I've never seen such a smart person. Big Sis Mimir said that having a lot of knowledge and being able to match the other person's level to explain in an easy way were a completely different thing. But since Ilysses can do both of them, he's a genius!"

Leonhardt nodded proudly. It always happened when Elizabeth learned something new, but this time as well, her face was flushed red like a newly ripe cherry. Mimir teased Elizabeth again, saying how she couldn't recognize her at first. Elizabeth had left for the seaside as a child and returned a lady that looked like she had received a blessing from the sea.

Elizabeth's laughter echoed like the rush of white-capped waves.

"What are you having so much fun talking about?" Ilysses was coming closer with a warmed-up kettle in his arms.

Seeing the way he carefully filled up all the empty cups, Leonhardt inwardly nodded in satisfaction. *He's a bit timid right now, but as long as he grows up this way, he will be someone who knows how to yell when he needs to... He has a good family, and he didn't seem to have gotten hurt in the meantime I didn't see him. Is his body still weak? I should feed him better.*

Without Leonhardt knowing, Ilysses had been so pressured at the Crown Prince's intense gaze that he tried his hardest to not look his way.

"I heard that you were talking about the tale of the mermaid. If you don't mind, can I also listen to it?"

"Oh, yes! By all means. So..."

Seeing how your face turned so bright in front of something you like, I guess you are also a child after all, Leonhardt thought as he rested his chin on his hand and smiled.

Unlike Mimir, who carelessly listened to Ilysses talking like she was listening to music, Elizabeth was completely immersed in his story. If what she knew so far was a puddle of water, the shy new friend in front of her had knowledge as wide and deep as a lake. Elizabeth was really fond of Ilysses. She thought how it was a different like from the like she felt for Leonhardt and the like she felt for Big Sis Mimir. She nodded at him as she listened.

Leonhardt was watching Elizabeth. Seeing her becoming a little more honest about her feelings, a rush of relief came like a breath of fresh air.

But why are Lizzie's earlobes turning red? Leonhardt tipped his head. Maybe she was too focused on his story, or the room was too hot... was what he could've used to brush it aside. But he felt a simmer in his chest that was growing to a boil.

CHAPTER FIFTY-SEVEN

"Come to think of it, we have not announced my pregnancy to the people yet," the empress said as she leaned her back into the emperor's wide, reliable arms and fed him a grape.

The emperor nodded and stared at the ceiling, thinking. "Empress, which do you think would be better—another son or a daughter?"

"Whichever one it is, I just hope they come easily. I have gotten older, so it will be tough."

The emperor placed his hand above the empress' belly and talked to her in a soft voice. "You are right, my Empress." He spoke to the growing baby next, "Hey, I know you're listening. Don't put too much strain on your mother, grow and be good."

As the emperor's arms were slowly moving side to side like a swing, the empress lightly closed her eyes and said, "By the way, we will have to gather the nobles again to announce the news... I hope we don't have a repeat of the welcoming reception."

"Ahem... ahem... What happened back then... No, it's nothing, Empress. Please just look, hear, and think of only good things." The emperor cupped the empress' face and turned it toward him in a hurry. "The thing you like the most is right here. Just think of me, I mean. Let us just think about how we should hold the party. That will be the best prenatal care."

The empress stared at the emperor with her round eyes and then laughed, nudging his chest with her head.

"It will be a flawless event. I promise."

"Of course. As it should!" the empress replied, poking the emperor's sides.

"Anyway, I wonder if it'll be a prince or a princess?" the emperor asked, feigning offense at the empress' attack and then leaning against her.

"Whichever is fine, I just hope they won't make the nannies suffer like Leon did when he was little." The empress went on about how it still gave her a headache to think about those days.

The emperor also nodded in understanding, bitterly regretting the mess that resulted from spoiling their first child. "But Leon, that boy, hasn't he been more mature and sensible these days? After hearing that he fought to death for the sake of his beloved, I saw him in a new light."

"That is true, but..."

"Empress?"

The empress hesitated for a moment before carefully opening her mouth again, "A child that always made us worry, one day started behaving like he was reborn in just a night... I am aware this might sound profane, but it feels awkward sometimes. To the point I start to wonder whether this child is really my child..."

The empress took a deep breath and a pause before she continued, "It is indeed good for a child who will one day lead the empire to behave maturely or become sensible early, but... how do I say this? Would you think the heat is getting to me if I say he was like an adult who had lived the world once and turned back into a child?" The empress knitted her eyebrows as she looked up at the emperor.

The emperor carefully patted the empress' back and closed his eyes. "Are you also under that impression, Empress?"

"It is not as much as my being under the impression. I'm just... just a little—very little—surprised."

The emperor opened his eyes and locked gazes with his beloved empress again. He then smiled and comforted her with his low and gentle voice, "Even so, Leonhardt is our one and only son. Is it not the saddest thing if the parents cannot trust their child? Even if he is up to something, it is only up to us as a couple to trust and wait for him. Don't you think?"

Only then did the empress' expression brighten up again. "It is as Your Majesty says. Well, seeing how he dedicates himself to his fiancée, Elizabeth, over everything, it's obvious he inherited that from Your Majesty."

"Is that so? Hmm, I am quite delighted that he got one of my qualities that I am most proud of. Then, what did he get from you, Empress?"

The empress widened her eyes again and opened her mouth in disbelief, scolding, "I think I have done everything I can by carrying him inside me with so much care for so many months. And now you ask what else I have given him? How greedy you are." The empress laughed lightly.

The emperor affectionately patted the empress' belly a few times and whispered, "I know you're listening from inside. Don't trouble my lovely Empress too much and come out healthy like the Crown Prince." The emperor's words overflowed with joy.

Leonhardt, listening outside the door with a servant, looked up at the servant in pity for always having to listen to such conversations.

The servant could only look at the pillar on the wall with a tearful face in front of the Crown Prince, who was starting to look like the emperor with his thick and distinct frame and fuzzy facial hair that was just beginning to form a mustache.

I came to talk to them about Lizzie's debut, but this timing is... Anyway, I guess a parent's intuition really is sharp. I need to act more... like a child, but... what was I like at seventeen years old again? No, my personality aside, I was already an emperor then. It's a bit ambiguous to act like a child again after all this time... It is my fault for not acting more cautiously. Now that it has come to this, should I just act like I'm a genius? No, no... Slowly... let's act slowly and carefully...

Still, it didn't feel too bad to look good while doing this and that for Elizabeth's sake. Leonhardt held back the rising corners of his mouth as the door to the emperor's bedchamber finally opened.

"Ahem, were you listening?"

Inside the room, Leonhardt said, "I shall continue to treat Lizzie well through what I see and learn."

"We really have to be careful with how we act in front of kids..." The emperor tutted and gave Leonhardt the side-eye for answering so craftily.

"Mother, how are you feeling?"

"It is not as tough as when I was pregnant with you, Crown Prince. I can still attend parties just fine, so you don't have to be too worried."

"Ugh... what did I do for you to say that?" Leonhardt scoffed. "I don't remember it at all!"

The empress chuckled after appreciating Leonhardt's flustered expression for a moment.

"You should check again to make sure that there is no mistake with the invited guests list."

"Hmm..."

The emperor gave Leonhardt an order, but it seemed like Leonhardt was thinking of something else as he rubbed his chin. The empress saw a trace of the emperor's youth when he did that, and she smiled inwardly.

"Father, please lend me your ear for a moment."

"Hm...?" Even though the emperor was skeptical, he tilted his head toward him anyway.

Leonhardt, with a mischievous expression only rascals of his age could make, whispered into his father's ears. The emperor's expression changed from a frown, to surprise, to a smirk. He patted Leonhardt's back. Leonhardt could barely hold his body back from stumbling as he grinned.

"I should take back my words saying that the Crown Prince has become too mature and sensible. Who knew the most wicked boy in this empire would be my son? You are completely prepared to kick those nasty nobles once you rise up to the throne, aren't you?"

"If that is father's long-cherished desire, of course, it is my duty as your son to do it. So, when are you going to give me the throne... Argh! father!" Leonhardt tumbled down the bed, fuming about what kind of father would kick his son like this. Scowling, he climbed back up to the bed.

"Seems like you are only now getting the punishment for kicking His Majesty everywhere, from his face to his legs, during your naps together in your childhood."

"Even you, mother...!" Leonhardt just shook his head. "This is why I have given up thinking this family should be the role model for the people. Anyway, did the painting change?" Leonhardt shifted his gaze toward the painting that was put up on the wall right across the bed. The painting had the emperor, the empress, Leonhardt, and Elizabeth with the sea as the background.

"I will also be calling over Miuccia for the party. Should I call any other people?"

"How about we let the people watch a play under your name while we're at it, Empress?"

"That is also a good idea. What do you think, mother?"

The empress smiled and nodded. "Let us take our time discussing the rest. Come to think of it, have you grown a little closer to Lord Perian?"

"Do you mean Ils?" Leonhardt tried to remember what happened in the last week.

"He wanted to learn magic from Mimir at first, but he had changed his courses to alchemy and science lately. Seeing how Elizabeth has been going to the library or the

Clock Tower with him, it seems like Ils has satisfied Elizabeth's curiosity quite well."

He's been with Elizabeth?

The empress and the emperor exchanged looks with each other.

"Is it all right for you to just watch like that?"

"Pardon?"

No matter how they looked at it, this foolish son of theirs didn't seem to recognize the gravity of the problem. No, maybe he was even too laid back. The emperor clicked his tongue like he couldn't believe he didn't know it before making another remark. "Crown Prince, you do remember that Elizabeth is still only your fiancée, don't you?"

"Pardon?" Leonhardt's brows rose.

The empress leaned on the emperor's shoulder as muffled a giggle, thinking that this reaction of his was a carbon copy of the emperor's.

Leonhardt's mouth fell open, stunned.

"Even though you've held your engagement ceremony, she is still not the official Crown Princess. Moreover, now that her debutante ball is approaching, maybe even the lady will..."

"L-Lizzie would never do that! And Ils is not that kind of guy!"

"Bystanders often pretend to be innocent, all while seeking the most vulgar and explicit forms of enjoyment behind the cover of their fans."

The empress nodded at the emperor's words. Leonhardt could only gape. Elizabeth and Ilysses... he never thought about it at all. Elizabeth had been his fiancée since before they were born, and they had already celebrated their engagement ceremony successfully. She would be his Crown Princess once they came of age, and once he became the emperor and she, the empress, they would live happily ever after as planned. But what if the person who could make that happily ever after happen was not him, but Ilysses?

Ilysses was the marquis of Perian's successor. That meant that although he couldn't make her happy the way a Crown Prince could, he could make her happy by other means. Comparing the imperial court's treasures and the empress' position with that of a marchioness, it was obvious that the latter could offer Elizabeth true happiness.

As their son's face stiffened and turned as white as a sheet, the empress and emperor observed him with interest.

There's... There's no way it would happen, but what if Lizzie says she'd rather be with Ilysses instead of me...? Can I let her go? Now that the future had been changed, what should he choose if that were really the best thing for Elizabeth?

Needless to say, he should connect them—at least for the sake of Elizabeth, who would get her engagement broken by the Crown Prince even after holding an engagement ceremony, and his friendship with Ilysses. However, just imagining having to make them take each other's hands with his own hands made him feel nauseated.

Calm, calm down. At times like this, I should think rationally and logically like an adult... or not! At least in front of father and mother, let's behave like a child. So... what I must do now is...

"That's never going to happen! Both of you know perfectly well how much I like Elizabeth!" Leonhardt shouted, falling for his parents' teasing.

LEMON-FLAVORED WALTZ

CHAPTER
FIFTY-EIGHT

A carriage with the imperial family's symbol headed towards the duke of Elysium's residence. Upon hearing that the imperial family's carriage had passed the gate, the duke of Elysium dashed out the door, barefoot. The butler followed, a pair of shoes in hand, and cleared his throat repeatedly at his master's undignified behavior.

"Why aren't they here yet? They've passed the gates a while ago already, so why can't I see the carriage yet?"

"Calm down, master. As you know, there is quite a distance from the gates to the mansion..."

"Gah! There's nothing good out of having a wide garden and a large mansion surrounded by a forest." The duke of Elysium stretched his head out repeatedly trying to see better, pacing back and forth in front of the door. Eventually, he spotted the decoration of the carriage glistening in the sun from a distance.

The butler stopped the duke of Elysium from running down the stairs—disregarding all formalities—and received a thin envelope on a silver platter in his stead. As if their business was done, the person inside the carriage didn't come out to greet the duke—other than briefly holding out a gloved hand—before turning the carriage around in a hurry.

However, only the butler was lamenting about how the family he was serving had fallen to this extent after seeing that. The duke of Elysium was just grinning from ear to ear even though he should've been angry at the rude guest, who failed to keep their manners in front of a duke.

The thing on top of the butler's silver platter was definitely an invitation carrying the imperial family's sigil.

"Is that child, Isolde, holding a debutante ball already? How old is she this year?"

"The young lady is turning seventeen this year," the butler murmured to the duke as an answer, sighing.

Even after the imperial family was mobilized to take the young lady to the imperial palace and such an unspeakably humiliating accident happened in the welcoming reception, nothing had changed with the duke and duchess of Elysium at all.

Well, something changed. The duke had started drinking himself to sleep every day and wearing strong-smelling perfume to mask the scent of alcohol.

And that was not all. It seemed that the duchess was still having nightmares about the rat coming out from her hair, leading her to wash her hands and bathe multiple times a day.

Thanks to that, the duchess' hands developed eczema and became rough and cracked, just like the hands of the maids who had to work without gloves in the middle of winter.

It was a wonder why the duke and duchess didn't realize that the more they tried to cover it with toxic perfumes and oils, the more they emphasized their own hideous traits and reminded the servants of what happened that day. Even just this month, there had already been five servants who left because they couldn't bear it anymore. They used to have hundreds of servants, befitting a ducal family, but now there were only a few left, just enough to maintain the mansion and attend to the duke and duchess.

Relieved that Lady Elizabeth was spared from witnessing this, the butler hurried back inside before the duke became hysterical again. As long as he was still the butler, it was his job to clean up the duke's study, which was becoming increasingly cluttered with bottles of alcohol frequently cluttered.

Without any idea what the butler was feeling as he gathered the bottles and spread black tea grounds on the carpet where the smell of alcohol was the strongest, the duke of Elysium entered the study, clutching the invitation as if it was a family heirloom. He demanded, "Where is my wife?"

"She is taking a bath, Sir."

"Again? It's already the third time today! Tell her to hurry up and come to the study because we got an invitation from the imperial court."

The maid who got the news from the butler carefully spoke to the duchess, "Madam, the imperial ..."

"Imperial court? What's with the imperial court?! Are they finally going to find fault in the fact that a rat came out from my hair? Or are they going to bring a charge against that foolish man?"

"An invitation has arrived, so the master instructed you to go to the study, madam."

The duchess stood up, became dizzy, and—because she had been soaking in the hot water too long to escape the thoughts of rats—collapsed. The maids helped her up and helped her get dressed, as they were used to.

The Elysiums who were revered as the Descendants of Angels no longer existed in this residence. Except one.

"The emperor clearly wrote this himself."

"It must be the emperor's handwriting itself! I am sure it must contain good news. This is not the time for this. Shouldn't all members of our family listen to this happy news?"

"You are absolutely correct, wife. You there, go and get Ludwig!"

The maid hurried and brought over a baby still in his swaddling clothes from the room Elizabeth used to stay in.

"Okay, Ludwig, look at this. It seems like your older sister is going to bring our family to glory once again!" The duke fluttered the thin paper in front of his son—who he was just seeing for the first time in weeks.

He was a lovely boy, with thin silver hair resembling dandelion fluff that seemed ready to fly away, and blue eyes that had only recently begun to dart around. However, suddenly overwhelmed with the stench of perfume and alcohol, Ludwig Mort von Elysium scrunched his eyebrows and started whining.

After a short moment of reading the room, the maid who brought Ludwig immediately started trying to calm him as she took him as far away from the duke as possible. Fortunately enough, Ludwig was always a child who was strangely quiet and seldom cried. He calmed back down as soon as the maid patted his back.

"That little fool who can't even recognize his own father..." The duke didn't consider his own body odor and only blamed the delicate newborn baby's sense of smell. No one in the study dared point it out to him.

"Darling," the duchess muttered, "Ludwig is still young after all... Rather than that, come, let us read what is written inside that invitation!"

"Ahem... Let's see, '*Dear Duke Elysium—I mean, in-law...*'"

There was a round spot that was especially large because the emperor pressed his pen on the paper too much as he pondered whether he should write this sentence or not.

"'*Dear! In-law!*' he said! The beginning is, well... not so bad, I'd say."

The duke was smiling already. He read, "*How is the situation at the duke's residence, surrounded by a forest in the middle of a hot summer every day? It feels like I can hear the sound of the bugs from all the way here in the imperial palace.*"

"How thoughtful of His Majesty! I did not expect that he would care so much about the state of our residence." The duchess interpreted it positively—even though it was meant to imply suffering, along with the presence of flies, moths, and mosquitoes.

"*I implore you to not be upset at the fact that I have failed to report how your daughter is doing to you, who are always in your residence only. This summer, all of us, including Lady Elizabeth, went to the empress' hometown. Think of the fact that she had fun and was so happy there as a consolation for not being able to tell you how she has been doing so far.*"

To be precise, the one who made them go under house arrest was the emperor. Also, the content under it was obviously saying that Elizabeth was much happier without her parents. However, the duke and duchess were already moved to tears and kept on chanting Isolde's name like a prayer.

"It seems like our Isolde is well-loved in the imperial nonetheless."

"Shh, the real content starts from this point. Let's see... the empress has conceived? What does this have to do with me?"

The butler and maid raised their heads up in surprise. It wasn't merely the news of someone conceiving; it was that of the empress herself. It was a matter that everyone should step in to celebrate, but the man who had forgotten his duty as the duke during his house arrest just stroked his mustache and read through the next paragraph.

"And that is why we are planning to hold a celebration for the empress' pregnancy and Elizabeth's debutante ball at the same time. She is still young, but I think it is time to hold it since we have already held her engagement ceremony."

"Our Isolde as a debutante! It must be saying that we shouldn't refuse and come since it's an event her parents must attend, right?" The duchess clasped her hands, looking elated.

But the duke didn't say anything.

"Darling?" The duchess touched the duke's shoulder.

The duke's arms that were stretched up in the air fell down, the piece of paper in his hand fluttered to the ground.

As the duke staggered backward, his rear touched the desk, and he slid down and dropped to the ground just like that.

While the butler was startled and immediately helped him up, the duchess picked up the fallen paper with trembling hands.

"Isn't the best prenatal care to look at nice things, hear nice things, and think nice things? Instead, I have laid down the order to relay you the news about the debutante through a painting. You must be disappointed and upset, but I believe you will understand my feelings."

Even the duchess' mind, which was usually able to positively interpret any sarcasm, went blank in the face of the emperor's explicit order not to attend. Written in his personal handwriting. The duchess' face turned pale and then blue.

"...Isolde... that... ungrateful... unhelpful little thing... So, she's abandoning this family in the end, after all!" The duke rose up from his position and shouted like an angry bull before starting to hurl everything in sight.

The maid turned her body around in a hurry and covered Ludwig's ears while anxiously waiting for the duchess to quickly lay down the order to take the child out of the room.

However, the duke snatched the emperor's letter from the duchess' hand, approached Ludwig, and yelled at the child who was still sensitive to all stimulation.

"Ludwig! Look! To think the wench who is your older sister would be this ungrateful! Only you... only you must never be like that! You are the successor of the Elysium family! You have a duty to revive the family! Stop crying this instant! Damn it, what are you doing not coaxing him? Everyone, get out of my sight!" the duke shouted, ripping off his shirt buttons that had been suffocating him in his fury.

All of them, except for the duke, thought this was the right time to exit the study. The duchess didn't even glance at her son, who was so frightened by his father, and just gestured for him to be taken away.

She went back to her room, muttering, "My hair... I have to wash my hair... There is no rat in the house, is there? I can find out as long as I brush and brush my hair with the thinnest and finest tooth comb..." The imperial court. Debutante ball. With only those words, she was brought back to the nightmare that had happened at the welcoming reception just a few years ago.

The butler could only sigh, standing in front of the study door, worrying about the goods of the mansion that the duke was destroying. Whenever the duke was dead drunk or encountered something unfavorable, he would react by smashing a perfectly fine chair, flipping the desk, or flinging anything on the desk to the ground, often several times a day. The butler, who had been serving the Elysium family for generations, had a gut feeling that he might be the Elysiums' last ever butler.

In the study, the duke ranted, "What do they think I've been hiding Ludwig's birth for?! What?! I was planning to show up in high society with my head held high when that child Isolde restores our family's name! Damn it... If I knew it would be like this, I would've told Isolde when Ludwig was born and entered the imperial palace... That incompetent daughter! A heartless child who won't even tell the emperor that she misses her parents! This is the end for Elysium... This is really the end...!"

He slouched in the middle of the study, now in shambles, tipping back the bottle of alcohol he had hidden. Cursing the imperial court and Elizabeth, duke gulped down the bitter liquid, taking another swallow with every piercing thought of resentment.

CHAPTER
FIFTY-NINE

Debutante ball.

That was the one day that all girls in high society dreamed of. The day the innocent and lovely young ladies, who had been raised dearly inside their parents' glass houses, came out into the world for the first time in their lives. On that day, they must shine brighter than anyone in the world.

However, with Elizabeth Isolde von Elysium's attendance, it was basically already decided who would shine the brightest at this year's ball.

At the gathering of the wives of high society, although they felt sorry for all the young ladies who had to give the brightest spot to Elizabeth, they were also looking forward to seeing if there was someone who could shine brighter.

"Leon will surely be my cavalier, right?" Elizabeth asked as if she had just remembered.

The tailor pinned another fold to demonstrate, gesturing at one of the scattered dress designs, concentrating.

Leonhardt nodded as if it was obvious. "Who else would do it if not me?"

"Umm... Bailey?"

At Elizabeth's sincere response, everyone turned their heads around to hold in their laughter.

Leonhardt plopped himself beside her and pinched Elizabeth's cheek playfully. "You want me to get Bailey to have a formal attire fitting right now?"

Elizabeth tried to imagine Bailey jumping around in excitement in the imperial garden while wearing formal attire. "Will he keep it on for at least ten minutes?"

"That boy has grown so much bigger. I guarantee that it won't even take him five minutes before he rips it all apart and makes a mess," Leonhardt answered nonchalantly as he picked up one of the design drafts.

As the fiancée of the Crown Prince, Elizabeth must shine brighter than anyone else at this year's ball.

Gosh, mother... She won't even wait a little longer. Although he had racked his brain for all sorts of schemes against the duke, he found himself at a loss at what to do with Elizabeth, who still looked so young, as the day of the debutante was approaching.

Even though men shouldn't be meddling in the matters of women's dressing up, it was a different case for a man who would be the cavalier escorting his fiancée. Thanks to that,

Leonhardt had pushed back everything in his schedule to get fitted with Elizabeth today.

"Whatever you're wearing will become a trend in the empire, so it won't be good unless it's something completely new and never seen before."

"But don't trends come and go...?"

"That is true." Leonhardt glared at the design draft. The paper depicted a young lady with a beautiful smile and a dress in a never-seen-before design. Leonhardt tried to dig through his remaining memory the best he could, exerting himself to remember what kind of clothes the future Elizabeth usually wore.

"White..." However, the only thing he remembered was the white dress that Elizabeth wore when she drank poison in his stead and threw up blood. It would be better to say that she had been wearing a white cloud. All the details had been blurred out in his mind.

"Isn't the first dress usually white...?"

"No, it's nothing." Leonhardt shook his head and browsed through the design drafts again. "Lizzie is still young, so how about something that feels bright?"

Something like a fairy, I mean. Leonhardt thought as he pushed aside all the design drafts that seemed to be trying hard to make her look as mature as possible.

The tailor perked her ears up to listen to the conversation between the young Crown Prince and her muse, hoping to get some hints in between.

"Uh... after some thinking, it could be said that Lizzie is somewhat of an outlier... Isn't the meaning of debutante kind of... different for Lizzie? So, it would be better if Lizzie alone... Ugh, how should I say this? Wouldn't she attract more attention if she's the only one with a different feel?"

Even though I once browsed through mother's wardrobe when I was small! Leonhardt waved his hands in the air, as if he were trying to depict an abstract image that he couldn't quite grasp. Elizabeth and the maids could only tilt their heads, unable to understand what he was trying to say at all. "Other people are not my concern, so whether they go to greet father or meet each other's eyes, just leave them alone... Something that can make Elizabeth shine alone... Not just making her wear a pretty dress or pretty decoration... That's it! Class! Make her have a whole different class!"

"A whole... different class... is it...?"

Leonhardt, who stood up from his seat all of a sudden in excitement, nodded. "Come to think of it, Elizabeth, isn't your family said to be the Descendants of Angels? We can just pursue that kind of class that's otherworldly!"

"What do you mean we can? Should I go out to the ball wearing angel's feathers or something?"

"That seems like it'll suit you."

"This is not the time to joke around."

"I'm also saying this very seriously."

While Elizabeth and Leonhardt were butting heads and having some kind of adorable love fight, the tailor tapped her forehead and considered the suggestions. *A different class... Another level... Fairy... Angel... Feathers...* Scribbling, the tailor studied the sketches and then tossed down her pen. She grabbed one of the design drafts and began to trace over it.

She beamed, showing them, "If we follow what Your Highness said, how about something like this?"

"I told you, you're either an angel or a fairy in my eyes."

"Leon, did your eyes perhaps finally go bad after smashing your head against the wall every day?"

"You say that, but why are you blushing then?" Leonhardt asked. "Huh? Lizzie, you have to shine the brightest. I'm sure you know since you always see it every year, but there's even a saying that we must make a separate fund for a debutante when a daughter is born."

"Saying that doesn't suit Leon."

"Ahem, ahem. Excuse me... Your Highness? Lady Elizabeth?" Only after clearing her throat a few times did the tailor finally get their attention.

"This is what I came up with after following what Your Highness said. All young ladies dream about being the most beautiful, the most important, shining star of the ball. But since that spot is already taken by Lady Elizabeth this year, the other ladies would compete to be the most eye-catching among the others and become at least the second most popular."

"What exactly does a debutante ball mean to those people that they're making such an uproar over it?" Elizabeth muttered in disbelief as she took the draft.

On paper was a lovely angel with small wings on her back and, atop her head, a halo with a golden chain. As if a jewel powder was floating on it, the silk woven with sparkling dew was loose yet naturally creased. Some gemstones were attached to the hem of the skirt to reflect light...

Leonhardt leaned his chin on his hand and leaned his back on the sofa with satisfaction.

"To give their well-raised daughters away in marriage to a great family. That's the real reason." The tailor began telling them how deep and dark the debutante ball was beneath its radiant cover.

"Give them away... in a marriage?"

"The young ladies might be giddy with expectations of meeting a prince or knight of their dreams, or a fateful love, but..."

"That's enough." Leonhardt cut the tailor off.

"Lizzie is still young." The tailor bent her waist in apology.

Elizabeth could only look around in confusion at the sudden mood change.

"Then, I shall look for other design drafts. Please excuse me." The tailor took all of the design drafts she had brought and left the imperial palace. If the Crown Prince hadn't stopped her just then, she would've made a huge slip of the tongue. Calling it a high society debut was just putting it nicely. It didn't have to be said that it was actually a marriage market for the adults who wanted to make an alliance under the guise of marrying their daughters into a good family.

The biggest victim of such a marriage market was Elizabeth after all.

Even so, I'm glad that all of her scars have disappeared, and she grew up so bright and healthy beyond recognition.

When they had first met, she had had so many scars. She hadn't even been able to pick out her favorite colors. Now, she could even play jokes with the Crown Prince without reservation and confidently express her preferences. The tailor, headed back to her workshop, thought it must be due to the effort of many people, but especially the Crown Prince.

"Why did you cut her off?" Elizabeth slipped in the question as she leaned her head against Leonhardt's shoulder. Leonhardt just kept playing with Elizabeth's hair in silence. "Hmm? Is it something I must not know about?"

"I'll tell you once you grow up a little more."

Elizabeth sat upright, annoyed at his unsatisfying answer. "How big should I grow though?"

Leonhardt asked Elizabeth to stand up. Within a few years, Leonhardt had grown up enough to make Elizabeth have to lift her head up slightly to look at him, even though he used to be a knuckle shorter than Elizabeth. Leonhardt placed his palm on top of Elizabeth's head and moved his palm towards his body while maintaining the parallel as much as he could. The palm touched right under Leonhardt's chin. "Once you grow as big as me?"

After seeing how big the gap was, Elizabeth puffed up her cheeks and scowled.

"Just have fun playing as much as you can while you're still young. Becoming an adult also means getting used to the shadows."

"Leon says that, but we are only two years apart."

"But I'm the Crown Prince. You don't know what I'm doing nowadays, do you?"

"Then is Your Highness the Crown Prince saying that you're already adult enough?"

"I am much more of an adult than Lady Elizabeth, at least."

"So, you must be able to eat bell peppers, carrots, and broccolis now, right?"

"Why are you suddenly talking about that?"

"I'm going to check it at today's dinner. I'm going to request it from the chef, so get ready!"

"Lizzie?" *I'm going crazy.* Leonhardt could only scratch his head as he was unable to keep up with Elizabeth bouncing away, here and there like a rubber ball.

Nevertheless, he was sincere in wanting her to remain innocent—protected—as long as possible. As long as she could spend every day joyfully, without worry, as long as she could smile like that, he would even wish for time to stop.

Without knowing that feeling of Leonhardt's, Elizabeth just smiled as she strolled away with the maids to head to the kitchen.

After being left behind with only Bailey, Leonhardt sat down on the ground before calling the dog over. Leonhardt let out a sigh as he stroked the weighty, fluffy warmth that came into his arms. He had already given up on himself because he never thought it was enough. No matter how many times he was given permission to be loved by her and to love her. But now he was at a loss for what to do with his young fiancée who said she liked him.

In the first place, the one she fell in love with was the nineteen-year-old Crown Prince who was always kind and gentle to her. Not the absolute fool underneath. If she discovered everything one day, would Elizabeth still say the same, would she still like him—love him—without reservation?

There was no way. No, she of all people could never find out. It felt like his personality had separated into two, making everything in his head more complicated.

Leonhardt buried his face into Bailey's cloud-like fur, letting out another sigh.

CHAPTER
SIXTY

While the tailor busily cut and sewed, the imperial gardener trimmed the flowers with neat workmanship, and the duke spouted treason in the privacy of his alcohol-scented study, Elizabeth and Leonhardt practiced dancing.

To be precise, it was less about dance practice and more a pair of young lovers playfully squabbling. Neither Elizabeth nor Leonhardt actually needed private dance lessons. Even so, they borrowed the smallest hall, allowing no one except Bailey to enter, and then started giggling inside.

"Stay still. You're trying to step on my foot again, aren't you?"

"But this is my first time doing the male dance steps. This is unfair. How come Leon can do it so easily?"

"Well, because I can just move the opposite of how I usually move...?"

"That's why I'm questioning how can it come so easily for you." Leonhardt hopped over to plop down on the sofa, checking whether the bone at the top of his foot was fine after being stepped on for the fifth time in a row.

"Are you okay? It's not broken, is it?"

"If my bone gets broken just because you stepped on it, it would have perished much earlier." Leonhardt said, pretending that tears weren't welling up at the corners of his eyes.

Elizabeth took off her dance shoes and sat on the opposite sofa from Leonhardt, stretching her legs towards him. Under the light skirt, her feet, covered only in white socks, were free to stretch. Elizabeth wriggled her toes, appreciating the sunlight making a lattice pattern on top of her feet.

Leonhardt had also taken off his socks and stretched his legs towards Elizabeth with his bare feet.

"You're more like a fairy queen than a fairy," Leonhardt said casually as he dropped his socks beside the sofa.

Elizabeth giggled as she poked Leonhardt's sole with her toe. "I don't like that. Titania and Oberon are separated, you know."

"I don't want to separate... What are you doing?"

Elizabeth, who was sitting with her back facing Leonhardt, glanced back before answering. "I want to be barefoot, too."

She proudly tossed her white socks away before stretching her legs out, smiling.

"Where did the most virtuous woman in the world I saw that day go?" Leonhardt muttered, unable to hide his bafflement.

Regardless, Elizabeth was busy giggling, wiggling her toes, and pressing her feet against Leon's, which were a few sizes larger than hers.

"Lizzie." After a moment of stretching and pulling each other's feet like they were playing a tug-of-war, Leonhardt called Elizabeth's name.

Elizabeth looked at him curiously.

Leonhardt faltered for a moment in front of the face that was so innocent and genuine, so trusting and filled with so much deep affection. He tried, "You know... if someone made a very, very foolish mistake and turned back time to fix that mistake, then succeeded in fixing that mistake and saving the person that was supposed to die because of his mistake... if that person loves him as a result... Is the one being loved the man he was before he turned back time, or is it the man who is living his second life after he turned back time?"

"Leon, did you get heat stroke?" Elizabeth pushed Leonhardt's soles all the way and blinked.

"It's just... I've been talking about that with Mimis Brunnr, you see. Like, what we would do if we turned back time."

"It's nice that it's showing your stature and dignity as the Crown Prince rather than smacking your head against the wall, but doesn't this hurt your head more?"

"Honestly, yes."

Elizabeth giggled. "Well... does that person know that their fate has changed because of the Time Traveler?"

"Hmm, no. I'll add the premise that they don't know."

"Then that Time Traveler basically wasted his time, no?"

"Wasted... his time?" Leonhardt tried to twitch his frozen face by any means.

Fortunately, Elizabeth didn't see his expression getting distorted because she was straightening her feet and bending her waist and head forward. "If that Time Traveler really wanted to fix his wrongs, then shouldn't he apologize first?"

Elizabeth straightened her body in a flexible movement like a cat before leaning back as much as she could this time. "You said the person died because of his mistake. If so, then I think he should apologize and say that he definitely won't be like that this time, and to prove that, show them exactly how he's fixing his mistake."

If not, then isn't he being utterly deceptive?

Elizabeth straightened her body again and tilted her head while saying, looking at him, waiting for agreement. Leonhardt didn't reply or do anything until the lattice-patterned sunlight on Elizabeth's feet moved towards her well-polished toenails. Even though Elizabeth was tilting her head, she waited patiently until he was done thinking.

"Hitting my head against the wall is much better than this. I really think this is the limit for my head," Leonhardt said at last, smiling awkwardly.

When Elizabeth thought of Mimis Brunnr and Mimir talking about metaphysical and philosophical topics difficult to understand among non-magicians unless they were more educated than the average person, and how Ilysses could join their conversation without any difficulty, she nodded. She then held her hand out to Leonhardt, who was frozen stiff, stuck in his head.

"Huh?"

"Let's dance, Leon."

Once Leonhardt realized that a pair of small, fair hands were extended toward him, he placed his hand on top of hers. Elizabeth pulled him up with all her might, and Leonhardt steadied his waist to help. They stood now close enough to feel each other's breath.

For a moment, an awkward silence took over. This place was definitely the smallest hall, but to the two of them, it felt wider and more spacious than the great hall they used for imperial balls.

Leonhardt, who ended up standing on the marble floor of the hall, placed his hands on Elizabeth's waist because he felt chills rising from his feet all the way to the top of his head.

"What are you doing?"

"Your feet will freeze." Unlike his curt reply, Leonhardt placed Elizabeth on top of his feet in a careful movement, like he was moving a flower from one vase to the next. Thanks to Elizabeth's bare feet being safely placed on top of Leonhardt's feet, she could escape from the cold marble floor.

However, it didn't seem like she was going to feel the cold anyway even if he didn't offer his feet as a replacement for her shoes. That was how much Elizabeth's face was turning red.

"Let's—dance." Leonhardt lightly wrapped his arm around Elizabeth's waist and extended his other hand under hers.

Elizabeth nodded and took his hand. Leonhardt hummed a waltz with a low voice, beginning the steps with Elizabeth's feet atop his own. The sun, observing the two of them across the lattice, craned its neck and began to appreciate their dance a little more.

Leonhardt was the wave and Elizabeth, standing on his feet, was the white boat. The sea embracing her had the softest sway in the world.

Was she dreaming? The summer sun had warmed up the velvet sofa to a temperature that was just right for a nap, so she might have just fallen asleep right there if she had laid down for a moment. She was dreaming. It had to be... to be something like this.

Elizabeth formed that conclusion by herself. However, the movement that firmly supported and guided her was someone else's. With a dreamy look on her face, Elizabeth looked up at the boatman moving her body left and right. His features looked sharp at first glance, as if a severe hand had etched his face. Upon closer inspection, however, he had well-defined features and skin that had been sun-kissed from summer sword training. His eyelashes, so long and delicate, were cast slightly downward.

Because he was looking down and staring straight into Elizabeth's eyes. The violet eyes underneath the lashes changed shades of purple and amethyst under the shadows. She was the only thing reflected in his eyes. That meant that she was the only thing filling his sight as well. Suddenly shy, Elizabeth averted her gaze.

"Elizabeth." Leonhardt, who had grown a whole head bigger than her before she knew it, called out her name carefully. "Look at me."

The gentlest command in the world.

Without realizing, Elizabeth turned her head back to him and lifted her chin towards him.

Whenever she took a breath, Leonhardt could feel a gust of warmth tickle his jaw.

Why did I only realize now? Why did I only realize after I lost her? She died without even being able to close her eyes properly, so why did I never try to look into her eyes? With all of the malice in the world, Leonhardt hurled curses at his future self, who had become the past and was gradually disappearing from his memory. An utter fool.

"Elizabeth."

"Yes, Leon?"

"Are you looking at me?"

"I am."

"Am I there, at the place you're looking?"

"It's filled with Leon."

"Are we looking at each other?"

Leonhardt was caught off guard for a moment when Elizabeth slipped her weight on her heels. She then got off his feet and hugged him.

"No, we're too close now. We can only look at each other's backs."

At Elizabeth's answer, Leonhardt firmly shook his head. "Not our backs, Lizzie. I am looking at you right now. I'm looking at the world where you exist. You're the entrance to the world I'm looking at as well as its only window I'm looking through."

Elizabeth leaned her forehead against Leonhardt's chest and chuckled. Even a sword master found himself sweating dancing under the sun with a lady soon to have her coming-of-age celebration.

Or maybe it was because she was his only sun—cliché as it was, it was the truth.

In any case, Elizabeth liked the body scent that came out of Leonhardt, and she kept inhaling and exhaling his scent. It was as if a part of him could become hers if she continued to do that.

"Leonhardt." After taking a deep breath and breathing out for the third time, Elizabeth lifted her head. Leonhardt's expression shifted as if he was a boy caught causing mischief. "I like you. I really like you. I'm so glad that Leon is the door of my world."

Her silver hair became a soft blade that cut through the sunlight, making a large part of the summer sunlight look like wings. With that summer sun on her back, Elizabeth smiled that certain way that made young Leonhardt doubt his eyes.

Elizabeth brushed her fingers across Leonhardt's face, confirming he was real, and not some dream or perfect sculpture. Carefully, she stood on tiptoe and leaned up for a kiss.

To be continued...